SON OF A FAST GUN

Hascal Giles was born in Big Stone Gap, Virginia on July 30, 1922. He was educated in public schools in Big Stone Gap. His first job was as a sports writer for the *Kingsport Times-News* in 1942. Giles began writing primarily Western short fiction for pulp magazines in the wee hours of the morning once the newspaper was put to bed. He became serious about his pulp writing but was no less serious about his career as a newspaperman. In 1948 he decided to try his hand at making a living freelancing. Giles started writing feature novelettes for Range Riders Western and Masked Rider Western and began expanding his pulp novelettes into novels that he sold to lending library publishers such as Arcadia House. *Kansas Trail* (1956) was his first original novel for Ballantine Books. Over the years other novels appeared, like *Texas Maverick* (1990) *Texas Blood* (1992). They are stories imbued with moral dilemmas, emotional suffering, and the achievement of wisdom as the result of extraordinary, even shattering, confrontations with the best and worst in human nature. The dominating themes of his fiction are the twisted tapestry of the past revealed in the present through the harsh light of psychological revelation, the examination of the false premises and moral weaknesses that produce so much anguish and misfortune in life, the explosive sexual aspect of the love a man and a woman can have for each other, the importance of family and love, and the ultimate need to be able to forgive and to learn from conflict. They are themes that will long retain their intense relevance and also reward the interest of anyone who happens to come upon a story carrying his byline.

SON OF A FAST GUN

Hascal Giles

GUNSMOKE

This hardback edition 2009
by BBC Audiobooks Ltd
by arrangement with
Golden West Literary Agency

ISBN 978 1 405 68285 5

British Library Cataloguing in Publication Data available.

Printed and bound in Great Britain by
CPI Antony Rowe, Chippenham and Eastbourne

Chapter One

Ed Jessup was still five miles from the town of Singletree when the two riders came pounding up behind him. One of them called his name. He slowed the buckskin and twisted in the saddle, squinting to identify the figures through the swirling dust. A scowl touched his face and he brought the horse to a halt, turning to face Sam Ditmar and Harve Grayson.

"Whew!" Sam Ditmar exclaimed as they drew abreast. "I'm sure glad we caught you before you got to town."

Ditmar's thin, dark face was lined with concern, and he swung his glance toward Harve Grayson as though he needed support.

"I hope nothing's happened to my pa," Ed Jessup said, watching the men curiously. "He hasn't been acting like himself lately."

Harve Grayson lifted his worn black Stetson and mopped the sweat from his bald head with a red handkerchief. "He's showing his age some, I guess, but he seems the same Jericho John Jessup to me. We knew this was the day you was to meet that cattle dealer in Singletree, so we came by your spread hoping to catch you before you left. Jericho John said you'd already lit out for town. That's why we're here."

Ed was surprised by their arrival. "Are you going to buy some of Wally Ogden's Hereford cattle, too?"

"No," said Grayson. "We don't know nothing about them new breeds of cattle. We don't want to know. No, we didn't ride this way to buy cattle. We're here to stop you from making any kind of cattle deal right now."

Ed Jessup folded his hands firmly on the saddle horn. There was determination in the set of his square brown face and resentment in the level blue gaze. "And how, good neighbors, do you figure to do that?"

"Like this!"

Sam Ditmar's voice, tight and nervous, came to him from the left. They had talked along the trail, and they had made their plans. Sam Ditmar sat straight and tense in the saddle with a loaded .45 Colt aimed at Ed's chest.

"Sorry, son," Harve Grayson murmured. Ed swung disbelieving eyes from one to the other. "We knew you'd be stubborn about this, but so are we," Grayson said.

"Sorry, hell!" Ed Jessup exploded. "It's not going to be that easy, Harve. I can't believe you two hombres are doing this. You two got a toehold on Maverick Creek by hanging onto my pa's coattails, and now you're aiming to kill me to keep me from riding into town to handle my own private business?"

Ed snatched angrily at the buckskin's reins, but his hands froze at the snapping sound of a six-gun going into full cock.

"We'll knock you out of that saddle with a bullet if we have to," Sam Ditmar said. "We didn't say we'd kill you. We just want to keep you out of Singletree until that cattle dealer gives up and leaves town. It's not just your business, Ed. When you go up against Morgan Hill it involves everybody on Maverick Creek. That's

6

you, us, and some others. We don't want a war with the Skillet Ranch. Hill has left us alone up to now, and we want to keep it that way."

"I never pegged you for a coward, Harve. You must be more afraid of Hill than I thought or you'd never do a thing like this."

Ditmar's seamed face tightened. "I'm afraid of him . . . I admit that. We're all afraid of him — afraid of what he can do to us. I figure we've been left alone because Morgan Hill cottons to famous people. Your pa's a famous man, but you can push Hill only so far before things change."

Ed Jessup's gaze shifted from one face to the other. He no longer doubted their intent. They didn't like turning against a friend, but they would not back down, not when they considered having to face Morgan Hill and all the Skillet if they failed.

Even though their betrayal angered him, Ed could understand their concern. He had witnessed firsthand Morgan Hill's iron will. It was because of Ed's interest in Molly Hill that the rancher had sent his daughter away to a St. Louis boarding school for a year, hoping she would forget him and find other interests.

At the same time he had ordered Ed Jessup never to visit her again, stating coldly that his daughter would not be allowed to waste her life with a shirttail rancher.

"Let's get going," Harve Grayson said impatiently.

Ed tried to prolong the conversation, stalling for time and looking for a chance to catch the men off guard. His voice casual, he said, "Maybe it won't make any difference to Hill what I do."

"It does," Harve Grayson snapped. "Skillet's been branding cattle around Comanche Draw for a week or so. Me'n Sam dropped by there yesterday, and ran into Morgan Hill. We got to talking some about this

7

Hereford breed. I mentioned to Morgan that you was thinking on buying some breed stock to build up the Triple J herd."

"When you start meddling in another man's business you go all the way, don't you, Harve?"

Grayson ignored the jibe. "Morgan looked real upset when I told him your plans, started twisting on that big diamond ring of his like he was going to tear his finger off, then he said it looked like a bad market year coming on. He said grazing land was getting overcrowded in these parts. He said he'd advise folks to hold on to any money they have instead of going off half-cocked and trying to build up their brand. It's plain enough how he feels about all of us north of Maverick Creek."

For a moment, Ed Jessup said nothing. He raised his eyes to the blazing Texas sun like a man looking for storm warnings. The glance he gave the two men flanking him was akin to pity, but the hard, unrelenting sheen of defiance still smoldered in the pale blue eyes.

"All right," he said at last. "I reckon we'll just keep on acting like scared rabbits, even on our own land. What do you want me to do?"

"Ride back with us," Ditmar said. "It ain't a good day for you to be going to town, anyway. Your pa told us this is the day Molly Hill is coming back home from the East. Skillet will be there to meet the stage, and you'd be sure to run into Morgan Hill while you was buying them cattle. Maybe you'd run into Molly, too. It ain't a good day to be in Singletree a'tall. We'll ride back with you and talk to Jericho John together. Your pa can set you straight on this."

Ed Jessup's buckskin was facing back the way he had come. He lifted the reins and the horse stepped forward, passing between Ditmar and Grayson. It

8

seemed a natural move, but Ed's surrender was deceptive.

As he passed Sam Ditmar, Ed's left arm swung out with a resounding slap. The blow caught Ditmar under the ear, jarring his head. Ed's body followed the swing. He flung himself sideways from the saddle, going across Ditmar's horse. His arms encircled the slender rancher, and they tumbled to the ground together.

A thunderous roar exploded in Ed's ears as Ditmar's gun went off. He felt the heat of the slug pass close to his ribs, then he was reaching for the hot Colt, clawing, slashing and rolling aside. He sat up five feet away with the gun in his hand and a smear of dirt across his chin. Slowly, swiveling the Colt to keep both men covered, Ed stood up.

Stunned, Harve Grayson still sat in his saddle, his hands hard against his thighs, his mouth hanging open. Sam Ditmar clambered awkwardly to his feet. He had a sheepish look on his face.

They stood that way in silence for a minute or two, then Ed hefted the Colt tentatively in his hand and said, "Catch!" He tossed the gun to Sam Ditmar, who put it quickly in his holster.

"Don't ever pull a gun on me again," Ed said quietly. "I've been handling a gun since I was old enough to ride. Pa saw to that, and you're the ones who keep talking about Jericho John once being the fastest gun in Texas. Now you two ride on back to Maverick Creek, and let's go on being friends."

"Then you're going ahead with your plans?" Harve Grayson asked. His words were muffled by the bandanna he used to mop his face.

Ed nodded. "I'm finally going to try to build Triple J into a profitable spread, Harve. Pa is old and tired, and he never did know which way to turn because of Morgan Hill. I've been telling him how we should run

9

things, and now he's turned it all over to me and told me to do what I think best. Maybe drought and hookworms and low beef prices will beat me, but at least I won't have to be ashamed of that. I'll never be able to hold my head up if I let Morgan Hill tell me I can't make the most out of my own grass."

Sam Ditmar shuddered. "You'll get yourself killed, Ed. You'll get us all killed," he warned.

"We're already dead, Sam," Ed said. "Morgan Hill dug us a grave the day we moved in. He looks at us as just temporary owners, hanging on by his good graces. We can stay only as long as we don't try to get big enough to make a decent living. Either we ought to get in that grave he dug for us, and make room for somebody with guts, or run our spreads the way we want to."

Ed moved toward his horse, brushing dust from his Levis. At the side of the buckskin, he stooped and recovered the bone-handled .45 which had jostled from his holster. He blew against the cartridge cylinders, adjusted the gun in the holster, and stepped into the saddle.

For a moment, he sat staring at the ground, a sun-browned, compact man of medium height. Deep creases furrowed his brow and his wide shoulders slumped briefly, giving him the look of a man much older than his twenty-four years.

Just talking about the pressure Morgan Hill exerted on the small ranchers had dampened his spirits, filling him with the frustrating hopelessness he had experienced most of his life. Straightening up, he looked across at his two neighbors and his pale eyes narrowed.

"I don't want to cause trouble for anybody," he said, "but I don't aim to be Morgan Hill's lapdog. I hope you can understand that."

10

"I guess we do," Ditmar said lamely. As Ed rode away Harve Grayson called at his back, "No hard feelings, son."

There was an unusual amount of activity in Singletree for a weekday, but Monday was the scheduled arrival time of the weekly stagecoach from the East, and that occasion always caused a stir in town.

Ed Jessup paid little attention to the traffic as he rode along the dusty street. Some of the old-timers on the boardwalk called out his name or yelled a greeting, and Ed nodded in return. These were the ones who knew he was Jericho John Jessup's son, and they showed him a measure of deference because of it, but a whole generation had grown up who had never heard of his father's exploits, so the younger people gave him no special notice.

Midway along the street, Ed passed the Drover's Pride Hotel, a two-story, clapboarded building with a gilt sign on the large front window which boasted 14 Clean Rooms And The Best Food In Texas. The hotel was set back twenty paces from the other buildings on a large grassy plot of its own. A curving drive offered access to the front entrance from either direction so buggies and carriages could stop there without suffering the dust and clatter of the main street.

Ed slowed the buckskin, almost bringing him to a halt, when he noticed the shiny black carriage parked in front of the hotel. Two fine mares pranced restlessly in the traces. Ed would have recognized the rig, with its polished leather seats and crisp canvas top, even without any identification as Morgan Hill's. But Hill was proud of his possessions and he wanted no mistakes about who owned them. Emblazoned in white paint on the side of the carriage was a looping circle

11

with the stem running from the left side symbolizing the Skillet brand.

Nearby were two horses bearing the same mark. Ed knew that Hill and some of his riders were already here to greet Molly upon her arrival.

His face sober, Ed nudged the buckskin back to its pace. His destination was McPherson's Livery Barn at the far end of the street. There he was supposed to meet the cattle dealer at four o'clock.

A sense of anticipation warmed him as he studied the towering, arch-roofed barn with the protruding beam over the hayloft door. He could hear animal sounds and smell the odor of hay and manure which came from the corrals and cattle pens sprawled across the four or five acres surrounding the stables. Within an hour he would be the owner of a dozen blooded heifers and a Hereford bull, a transaction which would mark a new beginning for the Triple J Ranch.

In a money belt beneath his shirt, Ed carried a sheaf of bills which totalled $672, all the money he and his father had managed to accumulate in fifteen hard years of ranching. It was a substantial sum to pay for a few cows when longhorns were bringing twenty-five dollars a head at the railhead in Dodge, but within five years, with the natural reproduction level of cattle, he would have more than a hundred of the new breed. Triple J beef would be selling at a price no longhorn could ever match.

By the time he drew rein in front of McPherson's barn, Ed's excitement over the prospects of new prosperity were beginning to surrender to the knot of nervousness in his stomach. After months of planning, and the exchange of letters between him and Wally Ogden, the cattle dealer, the timing of their meeting had turned out to be bad. At the time the business date was arranged, he had no way of knowing Molly

Hill would be arriving in Singletree on the same day, or that Morgan Hill would have reason to be in town.

On top of that, he had not been able to put the incident on the trail out of his mind. Despite the bold front he had shown Sam Ditmar and Harve Grayson, Ed shared much of their apprehension. He too feared Morgan Hill's reaction when the rancher found out that Ed meant to expand operations.

At the front of the livery, Ed stepped down and looped the horse's reins across the tie-bar which ran along the front of the building. A handyman was sweeping chaff and dust through a doorway at the far corner of the barn, an indication McPherson was getting ready for the spring dance he put on each year for the young people around Singletree.

The lower level of the building on that end had a planked floor. At this time of year, the liveryman had already disposed of the winter hay stock which had been stored there.

The handyman looked up, nodded, and went on with his work. Ed started to call out to inquire about McPherson, when he saw the liveryman come through the broad opening which led to the horse stalls.

Adam McPherson was a squat, thick-waisted little man with a round face and a generous mouth which smiled most of the time. A widower in his fifties, McPherson was childless, but he had a way with the young people, and they flocked around him to joke with him and listen to his stories. It was McPherson who had called Ed's attention to the Hereford breed, showing him stories from a Denver newspaper which described the advantages they held over Texas longhorns.

Ed had been fascinated to learn the Herefords had come all the way from England, first brought into this part of the country by a wealthy Briton who had acquired vast land holdings in South Texas. They were built close to the ground—short-legged, heavy-shouldered animals which fattened quickly on Texas grass—and their beef was sweet and tender, unlike the strong stringy meat of the longhorns. McPherson had provided Ed with the address of the man who could supply them—a cattle dealer named Wally Ogden.

Now, as the liveryman trudged toward him, Ed took note that McPherson was alone. The characteristic grin he was accustomed to seeing on McPherson's florid face was absent. Ed was a few minutes early, however, and he guessed that Wally Ogden would probably show up soon.

In his letters to Ed, Ogden had said he would be driving a herd of seventy-five Herefords to the San Antonio region. He would pass within five miles of Singletree, and would rest the herd while he and Ed Jessup finalized arrangements at McPherson's Livery. After he was paid for the thirteen head he had promised, Ogden was to lend him a drover to help Ed drive the Herefords to the Triple J.

"I guess I'm early." Ed smiled as McPherson came up to him.

McPherson did not return the smile. The corners of his mouth drooped, and his round blue eyes reflected irritation.

"Early?" he said. "Ogden's done come and gone. He's moving them Herefords on south by now."

"I'm late?" Ed said in disbelief.

He glanced at the sun, which was midway past its zenith, pouring down its meanest heat of the day. Sweat dripped from the tips of the strands of black hair which had slipped from his hatband and were plastered to his dusty forehead.

"That man's timepiece must be running fast," he said. "It can't be four o'clock yet."

14

Shaking his head, McPherson drew a thick gold watch from his vest pocket. "Ten 'til, but Ogden made good time. He got in about two or three hours ago. There wasn't anything wrong with his timepiece—just something wrong with you."

"What do you mean?"

"You ain't rich enough—not rich like Morgan Hill. I'm sorry as hell about this, Ed. I feel to blame because I put you onto Wally Ogden. I've knowed him for years, rode with him on a place near the Trinity. I figured him as a man you could count on, but he's either afraid of Hill or likes his money. Either way drops him down a notch in my book."

Ed frowned. "What's Morgan Hill got to do with it?"

"Hill heard there was a cattle dealer at my place, so he sent one of his riders over to ask Ogden to meet him at the Drover's Pride Hotel. Ogden was gone just a few minutes. When he got back he said to tell you he couldn't spare any of the Herefords. He said he had just enough to fill his contract at San Antone, then he lit out. We both know what happened."

Anger flushed Ed's face. "Yeah, we know. Hill paid Ogden not to sell to me. I'd guess he gave him the price of the Herefords and let him keep them."

Adam McPherson nodded. "Hill don't aim to be crowded. He's never going to let the ranchers on Maverick Creek grow any if he can help it. If the herds up there get any bigger he figures they'll be using graze he might want some day. He's been edgy about close neighbors for a long time. You know what happened to that squatter—the one who run off with Hill's wife."

Ed was listening, but his eyes were not on McPherson. He was looking aside, his glance running up the street toward the Drover's Pride, where he had seen Morgan Hill's carriage. "Yeah, I know about that, but

15

we're not squatters. Pa's got better than seven thousand deeded acres bought and paid for. We've got as much right as the next man to graze on the open range that joins our land. That's been done since the first rancher came to Texas."

"I know," McPherson said, "but Hill's had his eyes on that land ever since he run off the squatter. Al Burke was that bird's name — it just came to me. Hill never got around to buying up any land past Maverick Creek, but nobody dared touch it until Jericho John showed up. He wasn't about to mess with Jericho John, and you've heard how loco he is about anybody with a gun rep. He figured it was something special to have Jericho John as a neighbor. Something's changed, though. A year or so ago he wouldn't have risked offending your pa by cutting you out of them Herefords. Morgan's laid low a long time, but he's getting pushy now."

Ed tugged at his hat and turned to leave. He said, "If he pushes hard enough, I might just have to push back."

Chapter Two

Ed Jessup stood far back in the shadows beneath the wooden awning that sheltered the front of the Overland Stage office, his hat brim pulled low, the stub of a cigarette burning close to his clamped lips. Around him were a dozen other people, some murmuring in conversation, some pacing restlessly along the boardwalk and squinting against the glare of the sun-bleached alkali of the street as they scanned the horizon for some sign of the westbound coach.

He knew a few of the people, townsmen who kept businesses along Main Street, but many of the cowmen and riders from the sage flats south of Singletree were strangers to him.

"An hour late already," grumbled a man nearby. Ed was surprised by the swift passage of time. He stepped away from the wall to look through the grimy window at the clock on the rear wall of the stage office. It was half past five.

He turned to stare along the street himself as the sound of creaking harness and moving wheels attracted the crowd's attention. Morgan Hill's shiny black carriage came into view as the crowd shuffled about to make room for the rancher along the boardwalk. Hill halted the team, looped the reins around the brake handle, then sat waiting while the two riders who had accompanied him dismounted and tied their horses to the hitching rail behind him.

One of the riders was a wiry, weathered man Ed had heard called Thad Lawson. His companion, Brady Wayne, the Skillet foreman, was a man who attracted immediate notice in any crowd. He was Ed Jessup's age, but his flawless skin, dimpled cheeks, and wide brown eyes gave him the appearance of a handsome boy not yet old enough to shave. His hair was gold, and he wore it long so that it tumbled from beneath his big white Stetson and fell in waves over his broad shoulders. As he moved toward the carriage, sunlight flashed from the silver inlays in the black butt of the .45 Colt Wayne carried low on his right thigh.

The two Skillet men came alongside the carriage and Morgan Hill stepped down to join them. They stood a moment, talking quietly, and then the three of them moved up on the boardwalk to take advantage of the awning's shade. Ed backed deeper into the shadows, putting two or three people between him and the Skillet men as they stopped on the other side of the doorway only a few strides away from him. He had no business here, Ed told himself, and he had no intention of forcing his attention on Molly Hill. She had offered no protest when her father forbade her to see him again, and Ed was too proud to force the issue unless she gave some indication it was what she wanted.

He did not want to provoke Morgan Hill deliberately, but even his presence here at this time might be enough to anger the man. Ed scowled at the thought, drew deeply on his cigarette, then crushed it under his boot. Had Wally Ogden kept his word and sold him the Herefords, Ed would have avoided the temptation to watch the arrival of the stage. Instead, he would have been somewhere south of town, starting a herd of blooded heifers toward the Triple J Ranch.

Disappointment was so heavy within him he could not ride home just yet. His hand strayed occasionally to the folded letter he carried behind the sack of Bull Durham in his right shirt pocket. It had arrived a week ago. It did not convey any hint of affection, but it did indicate that Molly Hill had been thinking of him during the time she had been away.

When he'd left McPherson's, fighting his anger and dejection, he had realized it was time for the stage to arrive. As he rode over, he'd taken the faintly perfumed note from his pocket and read the neat, sweeping lines again. There were only a few lines, but he enjoyed imagining the sound of Molly's voice and the sight of her soft red lips as they moved with the words:

Dear Ed: For reasons we both understand, I know you can't be around when I arrive in Singletree, but I did want you to know I am returning to Skillet. I will be on the Overland which gets into Singletree on the afternoon of the fourteenth.

The letter was signed, "Your friend, Molly."

She was more than a friend—much more. Ed had known her since childhood, but it was only during the last year before she left that he had begun to feel he was in love with her. He could not judge the depth of Molly's feelings, however. Sometimes she was warm and affectionate, accepting his kisses and caresses with a hunger that filled him with desire. At other times she was cool and indifferent, and in the last few months before she went to St. Louis, he had seen her often in the company of Brady Wayne.

After reading her letter one more time, Ed had

19

been drawn to the stage office despite the voice of common sense, which told him it was not a wise move. He had to see her again, to hear her voice, to try to determine if an eastern education and new experiences in St. Louis had changed her. If he did not approach her, or speak to her in front of Morgan Hill and the Skillet riders, there would be no harm, he convinced himself.

From the moment Morgan Hill arrived at the Overland office, however, Ed had felt edgy and uneasy. He wanted to move farther away, but the wall of the building was at his back. There was no place he could go without attracting more attention than he would by standing still. Until this morning, he had not told his father about Molly's letter, and he had seen the worry in John Jessup's eyes as he left the ranch. It was the same deep concern he had seen in the faces of Sam Ditmar and Harve Grayson when they waylaid him on the trail.

They knew Morgan Hill had told Ed to stay away from Molly. Within a few days after his confrontation with the Skillet owner, word of the incident had spread across the Singletree range. Some of the ranchers had admitted frankly they had heard the story from Brady Wayne. Apparently the Skillet foreman believed that gossip would discredit Ed in both the eyes of Molly and his friends, lessening competition for the girl's affection.

Ed had never underestimated Morgan Hill's capacity for finding ways to punish those who offended him. He would never have ridden to Singletree for the sole purpose of meeting Molly. Such open defiance of Hill's ultimatum could only mean trouble. Hill had found out about the Hereford deal, and he knew why Ed was in town. Still, he feared Hill would not accept such logic if he thought Ed was pursuing Molly. It was a foolish risk, Ed decided. He cast a guarded glance toward the Skillet men, shrugged with resignation, and decided to leave.

He had taken only a step away from the office wall when he heard horses blowing air from their muzzles, and then came the crack of a whip. Off to his right, someone shouted, "Here she comes!"

Ed remained where he was.

A stooped, bearded old man jostled Ed as the knot of people began shifting and pressing toward the curb. The man looked up apologetically. "Better move aside a mite," he said. "Skillet is here, and Mr. Hill will want to be up front when the coach stops. Hear tell his daughter is coming in from the East."

Morgan Hill and his companions pushed through to stand directly in front of the office entrance. An aisle opened for them, and they accepted the courtesy in the manner of those entitled to such attention. Hill stood between Thad Lawson and Brady Wayne, towering a head above them. His expensive black suit was newly pressed, his white silk shirt only a shade lighter than his thick long hair, cut frontiersman style, brushing the collar of his coat. His hands were clasped across his middle, and he toyed impatiently with the big diamond ring on the little finger of his left hand.

People nearby were eyeing Morgan Hill with covert glances. He pretended not to notice them, but he was aware of their interest and liked it. He owned the biggest ranch between the Canadian and the Colorado, and he wanted everyone to be aware of the Skillet brand's prestige. The "Iron Skillet," Hill called it, a subtle boast that he expected his holdings to last through the ages. Hill was not a man who measured greatness by the span of his hand or the length of his shadow. But he could cover a lot of territory with either.

21

Hill's shadow lay over this whole section of Texas. It was the shadow of wealth and power — of land, cattle, and influence. At the moment, that tall shadow sprawled across the boardwalk in front of Ed Jessup, and Ed felt a desperate need to get away from it.

There had been a time, during the years he was growing up, when Ed had looked upon the tall, stately man as a friend. He was a stranger now, and it seemed a long time since Ed had looked directly at Morgan Hill's face. He looked at it now, a broad, sun-lined countenance which did not fit well with the fine clothes. There was a glint of bitterness in the hard gray eyes, the look of a brawler in the thrusting chin and tight lips. Much of the man's nature was reflected in his face if the tales Ed had heard about Morgan Hill's harsh discipline at Skillet were true.

While he was studying the man, Ed's heart skipped a beat. Morgan Hill swung around and appeared to be staring directly at him, but their eyes did not meet. The rancher had merely shifted his position to get a better view of the oncoming stagecoach. Ed tugged his hat brim closer to his eyes, trying to conceal his face.

He stood that way until the double team of horses pawed to a halt, rocking the yellow-and-green coach and stirring up a dusty breeze. All eyes were on the door of the coach now, and Ed was more at ease. He straightened as the driver looped his reins, called the station name, and stepped down to stretch his legs.

Ed's fingers found tobacco and papers in the pocket which held Molly's letter. He worked at building a cig-arette, spilling tobacco down his shirtfront, hardly aware of what he was doing until he noticed how his hands were shaking. He tossed the makings aside, his eyes on the door of the coach.

He heard Molly Hill's voice first, a carefree squeal of delight as she bent low to peer out at the crowd.

22

Then she was stepping down on the burlap-covered box which the driver had arranged to shorten the distance to the street. There was a rustle of crinoline and a hint of perfume in the hot, still air. Ed felt the blood pounding in his temples before he got a clear glimpse of her.

She was as fresh and beautiful as he remembered. Her wheat gold hair fell in glistening curls below a stylish blue bonnet. He remembered how her slanted green eyes could tease a man with hidden thoughts, and he was keenly aware of the way the pearl gray dress she wore emphasized the shapely lines of her figure.

A smile spread across Ed Jessup's face. He found himself nodding in satisfaction. He had seen what he came for, a quick glimpse of Molly, and it had been worth waiting for. He was ready to ride home now, and let time determine the direction of their relationship.

He saw Molly's eyes settle on her father's face, and saw her push through the crowd toward him. Then she swung her head around, and suddenly she was looking straight into Ed's eyes.

Ignoring her father's outstretched arms, Molly ran directly toward Ed. She stopped in front of him, her eyes sparkling, her hands reaching up to grasp his shoulders.

"My goodness!" Molly laughed happily. "What a nice surprise! I never dreamed you'd be here, Ed, but I'm glad you came to meet me. It makes me feel right at home again."

Ed's face colored. He pushed her hands away and opened his mouth to explain that other business had brought him to town, but did not get a chance.

Brady Wayne had moved quickly to follow Molly's path. He was only a step behind her, his little-boy face

23

burning with fury. "Scum!" he snarled at Ed. "You've been warned about this."

Wayne's left hand shot forward. He grabbed Molly's shoulder and whirled her roughly away. His right hand was moving at the same time, knotted in a fist aimed at Ed Jessup's mouth.

Ed saw the blow coming. He twisted his head just in time, and Brady Wayne's fist only skimmed the point of Ed's chin before it slammed into the log wall of the Overland office. A grunt of pain escaped Wayne's lips as he pulled back his hand, and then Ed's own hands were busy. He slapped at the Skillet man's face with an open palm, then bunched his muscles and drove his other fist into Wayne's belly.

Brady Wayne slumped over with a groan, his snow white Stetson almost on a level with his knees. Ed braced his back against the wall, raised his leg, and slammed his boot heel into the man's shoulder.

Brady Wayne's body sailed backward. He landed on his side almost ten feet away. Before he fell, he bumped into two men standing behind him, and the three of them hit the boardwalk together. They cursed as they fell, then there was a scurrying of feet and a rattling of spurs as everyone scattered to get out of the way.

Ed looked around for Molly. She was standing in almost the same spot where she had caught her balance after Brady Wayne had shoved her away. Her green eyes were half-closed, sleepy looking, and her lips were slightly parted, moist and glistening. She was like a woman engulfed by passion, and Ed was shocked by the thought that she was savoring an odd, sensual thrill from the violence exploding around her.

It was not over yet. Ed turned his head just in time to see Brady Wayne roll over, prop himself on one elbow, and grab at the fancy Colt with his free

24

hand. In one fluid motion, Ed's own hand darted down and up. He barely beat the man's draw. His .45 fired just as the sight of Brady Wayne's gun cleared the holster.

Ed had aimed at the man's gun hand more by instinct than by plan, and he was only slightly off the mark. The bullet struck the gun barrel with a dull clank, knocked the Colt from Wayne's hand, and sent it bouncing across the boardwalk. He heard the ricocheting bullet glance away and go whining in some other direction.

During the space of a clock's tick, his mind working as feverishly as his arm, Ed had assumed the slug sailed harmlessly toward the sky. It was not until he saw Thad Lawson pulling at the Skillet owner's coat that he realized a piece of the bullet had struck Morgan Hill. As the tall cowboy slid his hand underneath Hill's coat, near the left shoulder, Ed saw the ragged tear in the fine material which had been tailored to fit the rancher's massive frame. A rust-colored stain was visible on the white silk shirt a few inches from the base of Morgan Hill's neck.

Hill did not make a sound. He did not even flinch. He pushed Thad Lawson aside, mumbling something to him and stood stoically, his granite eyes boring into Ed Jessup's face.

A few feet away, Brady Wayne pushed to his feet, flicking his fingers to restore the feeling in them. His mouth sagged open in surprise as he followed the gaze of the crowd, saw the blood on Morgan Hill's shirt and the stunned look on Ed Jessup's face.

After a long, silent minute, Morgan Hill slid his hand beneath his coat and explored the area around his collar. Wet blood glistened on his fingers when he withdrew them. He stared at his hand, rubbed his fingers together a few times, and kept looking at them as though he did not recognize the stain.

He looked again at Ed Jessup. His deep voice was soft with shock as he said, "You shot me, Jessup. No man has ever shot me before."

"No, sir, Mr. Hill. I didn't shoot you. It was an accident." Ed's face was hot, and he felt like choking fingers were cutting off the air from his lungs. "You'll have to blame your own man for what happened. Brady Wayne had no cause to try to kill me. My bullet must have split apart when it hit Wayne's gun. It was a ricochet, Mr. Hill, a pure accident. Looks like it just broke the skin a little. I'm sorry it happened."

The explanation was a waste of time. Ed had the sinking feeling he had committed an offense for which there was no forgiveness. Morgan Hill gave no indication he had heard Ed's voice. He continued to stand stiffly erect, his gray eyes hard and unblinking.

Molly rushed up beside him. She grasped the hand on the opposite side from the wound, and lifted it briefly to her lips. She did not look again in Ed's direction.

"You shot me," Morgan Hill repeated. "Right out here in — in front of half the town."

Ed took a step forward, holding out a placating hand as he tried to think of a more convincing apology, but Morgan Hill was not looking at him anymore. Abruptly, the Skillet owner turned and walked inside the stage office, his jutting chin giving him the look of an angry bulldog. Molly went with him, still clinging to his arm. Brady Wayne and Thad Lawson quickly followed them inside.

When he turned to leave, Ed saw that the rest of the passengers had not yet disembarked from the stagecoach. The driver, with wry humor, called out, "All of you can step down now. Our little celebration is over."

It seemed hours ago that Molly Hill's pretty face

had first appeared in the doorway of the coach. It had been only four or five minutes, but they were the longest, loudest, most fearful minutes Ed had ever known.

Just as he reached his horse, he saw the slim, stoop-shouldered figure of Dan Plover, the town marshal, emerge from Clayton's Saloon. The saloon was less than a hundred feet from the Overland office, and Plover could not have failed to hear the explosion of Ed's gun, but the marshal was not inclined to venture too close to trouble while it was in progress. He paused on the boardwalk, wiped a skinny hand across his lips, and swung his gaze along the street. He walked toward the stage office, paying little attention to the man climbing aboard the buckskin nearby.

Ed was equally indifferent to the marshal's presence. It was through Morgan Hill's influence that Dan Plover held his job, and the marshal would do whatever was needed to please the Skillet owner. If Hill ordered it, Dan Plover would put Ed Jessup in jail on some charge, but the Skillet owner would never permit the lawman to interfere in a personal matter. Morgan Hill tackled his own problems and settled his own grudges. Knowing this worried Ed more than the sight of any badge ever could.

Chapter Three

They caught up with him an hour after he left town, when he was less than halfway home. Ed Jessup was not surprised to see them. He first spotted them as they came out of a mesquite thicket he had passed through only a little while earlier. Morgan Hill had borrowed a horse somewhere, apparently leaving Molly in Singletree or sending her on to Skillet alone in the carriage.

The rancher was in the lead, riding a few yards ahead of Thad Lawson and Brady Wayne, who flanked him on each side. The horses were at full gallop, and they had been ridden hard. Even though they were nearly a quarter of a mile behind him, Ed could see the lather on the horses' flanks and hear their labored breathing.

Ed had not been misled by Morgan Hill's calm manner and quiet voice when the rancher turned away from him at the stage station. Men with wealth and power seldom rushed to settle an affair which has no deadline. They thrived on confidence, setting their goals with deliberation, then reaching them after careful planning.

Morgan Hill was such a man, and Ed knew he would not let the shooting incident pass without retribution of some kind. Ed had hoped it wouldn't come so soon, so he would have time to ride back to the ranch and seek his father's advice. The ricocheting bullet had wounded Hill's dignity more than his person, and it had taken a while for his anger to build, but fury would be goading him now, and Ed had no choice but to wait and face it.

He was in open country, surrounded by the grass and sage of the rolling prairie, which was beginning to take on hues of purple and gold under the slanting rays of the fading sun. Three miles farther on, where the prairie dropped to lower ground, the land was rougher, broken by twisting arroyos and a long, rocky draw which turned the trail northward toward Maverick Creek.

He could try to outrun the Skillet riders, seek cover in the badlands ahead, but that would serve no real purpose. Morgan Hill was determined, and he would continue the chase no matter where it might lead.

His nerves taut, Ed kept the buckskin at the same easy canter he had observed since leaving Singletree. He refused to show concern by looking back at the men, but in less than ten minutes they were abreast of him. He pulled his horse to a halt when they rode up, watching warily as the Skillet men established their positions.

Morgan Hill remained in the center of the trail, sitting stiffly erect aboard his borrowed black stallion. His face was the color of mahogany, filled with angry blood. He was not yet fifty years old, and even though his hair had turned prematurely gray, his thick eyebrows remained coal black, contrasting sharply with his granite gray eyes.

Ed shifted his gaze from one to the other. Brady Wayne danced his horse sideways, coming to a stop ten feet to Hill's left and slightly in front of him. Thad

Lawson, a pained look on his thin face, kept moving until he reined his mustang to a halt at Ed Jessup's back.

"You can't stay on Maverick Creek any longer!" Morgan Hill said. His voice was a rumble in his chest, and he spoke with the finality of a judge handing down a verdict from a hanging jury. "I've tolerated you folks a long time, but you've pushed me too far. I want you out of the country, and I want you out quick. Pass the word to Jericho John. Pack up and get out. You can't stay, so don't even try."

The arrogance of the man stunned Ed Jessup. He sat for a moment staring at Morgan Hill, drawing in deep breaths. It was unbelievable that any man, even a man like Morgan Hill, could assume he had the right to wipe out years of dreams, hopes, and hard work simply because he wanted it that way.

"We can stay," Ed said, anger thickening his voice. "We'll stay because it's our land, Mr. Hill, and you've got nothing to say about it. You blocked me on buying those Hereford stockers, but we've still got longhorns. Pa and I will round up every one we can find, and I aim to brand every maverick calf on the Triple J range to boot. You can't run me off my land."

A lift of the blocky chin, a stiffening of the brawny legs in the stirrups, were the only indications the Skillet owner had heard the defiant reply. He said, "You shot me. People will expect me to do something about that, and I aim to. If I let you stay around these parts it might give others some foolish notion they can push Skillet around and get away with it. And you're still running after my daughter, Jessup. I won't stand for that either. She's not going to team up with you and live like a Comanche squaw, working and worrying herself into the grave by the time she's thirty. Scum like you tore my family apart once, but it won't happen again. You've got till noon Thursday to get out of the country."

It was a lengthy speech. With it Morgan Kill spilled out the rage which had been simmering inside him since he saw the joy in Molly's face when she greeted Ed at the station — a rage which burned out of control after he felt the sting of a bullet from Ed's gun. He had held his temper in check while he thought about an appropriate course of action. He had reached that decision, and now there would be no compromise.

"You've let your own importance go to your head, Hill." Ed dispensed with the polite "mister," vowing silently never to accord the man such courtesy again. "You're not God, no matter what you think. You can't run a man off his land without so much as — "

"I can and I will," Hill cut in, "but I won't cheat a man like Jericho John. I've checked the records. Your pa paid a dollar an acre for most of his deeded land, a little more for some. There'll be a quit-claim deed and eight thousand dollars waiting for him at the Cattleman's Bank in Singletree. When you're settled, you can write the bank and the papers will be sent. You'll get the money when the bank gets the signed deed. That's the only deal I'll make. I want you out by noon Thursday, Jessup."

Turning his head aside, the rancher said, "You've heard what I told him. See that it's done, Brady."

"It'll be done, Morgan," Brady Wayne said. The Skillet foreman had been silent while Morgan Hill talked, but Ed had watched him from the corner of his eye.

Brady Wayne sat relaxed in the saddle, his wide brown eyes as expressionless as painted window glass. He had found another gun, and he rested his right hand only an inch away from the top of the open holster.

31

Ed could not fight Morgan Hill with words, and he had already discarded earlier thoughts about trying to chase the Skillet men away by force. They had him boxed in, Hill and Brady Wayne glaring at him from the front, Thad Lawson at his back.

Morgan Hill had spoken, and he expected the commands to be obeyed. He had given the Jessups two days to abandon the only chance Ed would ever have to become a secure and respected man, and he made it sound like a simple business deal.

Staring stonily at Morgan Hill, Ed yanked at the buckskin's reins and the horse responded with a quick turn. Morgan Hill's voice stopped him.

"Not yet," Hill said. There was a crispness in the tones that made Ed hold back his horse.

Morgan Hill claimed he had never acquired much skill with a handgun, and he seldom carried a pistol, but those who knew him well said he was a deadly shot with a rifle, and he was never very far away from one. Ed had noticed the Winchester in a saddle boot next to Hill's right knee when the rancher first rode up.

The Skillet owner now calmly lifted the rifle and aimed it at Ed Jessup's belt. His dark brows were drawn so closely together they seemed to form a solid black line across his granite eyes. "You're thinking about staying and fighting me — I can see that in your face — but you'll go, Jessup. When I'm finished with you, you'll be ready to go. You'll never want to come back to this part of Texas and face me again."

Hill paused, his massive chest swelling, and then, like a man crying out for his life, he yelled, "Drag him!"

From the beginning, the Skillet men had known how this would end, and their reaction to Hill's command was immediate. A rope hissed through the air. Before Ed Jessup could defend himself, a loop encircled his body. Brady Wayne leaped from his horse, his gun drawn. He stood looking up at Ed, a vacant smile on his face, his long golden hair shining like burnished brass. Thad Lawson tightened the loop, pinning Ed's arms to his sides; then Lawson spurred his horse, putting its weight and strength behind the rope, and Ed was jerked from the buckskin's saddle.

He hit the ground so hard the wind whooshed out of him. His teeth jarred together. A searing pain shot through his head. Thad Lawson and Brady Wayne were hovering above him, using the slack of the rope to throw dally loops around his arms and legs, trussing him up.

Holding the rope tight, Thad Lawson reached down and lifted the bone-handled Colt from its holster. He tossed it into the grass where Ed's brown Stetson had rolled to a halt. Lawson's face wore a frown, pinpoints of black beard showing through his skin as some of the color drained from his cheeks. He looked up at the Skillet owner, who sat aboard the black stallion a few feet away. "You sure you want to do this, Morgan?"

"Drag him!" Hill repeated.

Ed lay helpless on the ground. Nothing he could say would change Hill's mind, so he remained silent. Until now, he had doubted some of the stories he had heard about Hill's style of punishment for those whom he thought had wronged him.

He had been told about a bronc rider at Skillet being dragged at the end of a rope because he had ruined a horse's mouth trying to tame it. Against Hill's orders, the rider had worked with a Chileno bit, the ugly piece of iron the Mexicans called a bear trap because it could clamp against a horse's jaw with enough force to break it. Later he heard about a cowboy suffering the same fate after he stole a Skillet saddle and swapped it to a drifter for a six-gun.

33

There was more movement about him, and Ed had no more time to think. He felt another rope tighten around his legs, put there by Brady Wayne. Twisting his head, he saw the Skillet foreman holster his gun and move toward his horse in a dogtrot, uncoiling more of the rope as he went. On the other side, Thad Lawson was climbing aboard his mount, rope in hand. They had him anchored between them like a sling.

"Hi—yi—i—i!" Brady Wayne cried, and the horses leaped forward.

At first the sensation was one of gliding, his body slipping through the prairie grass like a sled. As the horses gained speed, the burning started, the clinging grass searing his skin like a hot iron. From then on there was nothing but pain—ripping, tearing, stinging pain that tore at every cell in his body.

They went across the prairie at a slow gallop, two men on horseback, two ropes drawn taut, and Ed Jessup's body sliding, bouncing, rolling, and tumbling behind them. A hundred yards one way, and a quick turn—a hundred yards back, and another turn. All the while Morgan Hill sat in his saddle and watched, his hands folded on the pommel, his chin thrust forward while the granite eyes followed the movement.

Scores of small rocks were hidden beneath the grass. Ed felt them gouging into him, cutting gashes in his flesh. Most of his shirt was gone, leaving his back bare except for a few shreds of cloth which bunched up around his belt. At the second turn, his head struck a thick clump of dead mesquite roots. Bright flashes flickered before his eyes, and a waterfall roared through his head. Everything was a muddy gray for a while, but he could still feel the pain. Blood covered his torso and ran into his waistband.

Back and forth they went, always turning where

Morgan Hill could have a clear view of them. Ed lost count of the trips across the grass. His mind was foggy, his vision blurred, and he wished for unconsciousness so the terrible pain would go away. Once he thought he heard a strange sound in the distance, then realized it was his own voice crying out in misery. He forced his mouth shut, biting his tongue, ashamed he had shown such weakness.

Finally, he heard another voice. The roaring in his head and the ringing in his ears made it sound like a distant echo, but it had come from Morgan Hill.

"That's enough!" the voice said. "I don't want him dead—I just want him to get out. Take the ropes off."

Afterward, he had a vague memory of saddle leather creaking, spurs rattling, and of hands touching him, but he did not know when the Skillet men left. He was a ragged, bloody, gasping heap on the ground, and he lay that way for a long time.

Dusk was creeping across the prairie when Ed Jessup tried to sit up. His stomach retched with nausea as the stretching of his skin opened the countless cuts and scratches across his back and shoulders. Dizziness spun the land around him, and he eased himself back to the ground. He lay on his back for a while, blinking and trying to gather his strength while he watched the first stars wink awake in the gray sky above him.

He flexed his muscles, trying to identify the worst of his wounds. His hands were not badly torn, but the knuckles were raw and he could feel dried blood between his fingers. The tough Levi's had provided more protection than the flannel shirt, but patches of skin had been peeled from his knees and hips, and the air passing across the exposed flesh was like the touch of a branding iron.

Again he sat up, taking deep breaths and swallowing hard. His throat was dry and his tongue felt thick and rough. The buckskin stood about fifteen feet away, stamping impatiently and cropping at the grass around its feet. On the other side Ed spotted his hat and gun. He did not hurry to pick them up. He sat staring, regarding the distance of a few paces as though it were miles, knowing the torture each move would bring to his body.

Rather than risk falling again, he crawled to recover the hat and gun, grimacing as his sore knees touched the ground. The activity helped to clear his head.

He pushed to his feet, bracing his hands against his thighs. With no one around to hear him, he did not try to hold back the low moans and soft curses that escaped his lips. Walking stiffly, he crossed to the buckskin. Somehow he managed to get into the saddle after two staggering attempts. He got the horse started along the trail, then lay forward on its neck. He felt sick again. There was blood all over him, and sweat bathed his body as the pain burned his nerves ragged.

It took him almost an hour to reach the rocky draw, but he did not turn with the trail which veered north toward Maverick Creek. He rode into the draw, eager to reach the cooling waters of the stream which ran along the bottom of the gulch at this time of year.

He loosened the horse's bridle and let it drink, then tore away the cuffs and collar of his shirt, which was about all that remained, and tossed them aside. Only when he started to wade into the water, still wearing the rest of his clothes, did he remember the money he had carried with him to buy the Herefords.

Ed's fingers slipped gingerly inside the slitted opening of the soft buckskin belt underneath his waistband. He sighed with relief when he found the money intact. Blood had oozed into the money belt, and the outer edge of the sheaf of bills was stained a rusty brown. Some of the bills were stuck together where the blood was beginning to dry. Ed spent a few minutes pulling the bills apart before he put the money inside his hat, which he had placed on a flat rock beside the stream.

Afterward, he went into the water, wading out until he reached a pool that rose almost to his waist. He squatted down, ducking his head to let the stream soothe the pounding pulse which throbbed at his temples.

He stayed in the water a long time. He felt some of his strength return, but his body was still tormented by pain. He inspected his chest and midsection for the first time. His upper body was a mass of fine red lines, interspersed here and there by deeper cuts where roots and rocks had dug into the flesh. He washed away as much as he could of the dirt and grass which was imbedded in the crusted blood, then he went back to his horse.

As he rode toward Maverick Creek Ed hardly noticed his surroundings. Looping the reins around the saddle horn, he let the horse find its way home. His mind was in a half stupor, but he found himself thinking about Morgan Hill's other dragging victims.

Around the saloons and shops in Singletree there were stories told about them, but no one had ever seen them, and now Ed understood why. When a man was rendered helpless and dragged across the earth like a slain animal he lost all trace of human dignity. Aside from the agony, it crushed a man's spirit and made him ashamed that he had allowed it to happen. Anyone without firm ties to this country would not risk suffering such humiliation twice.

Ed Jessup's punishment far exceeded his offense. It was Molly who had initiated the conversation at the stage station, and the bullet wound to Morgan Hill's shoulder was an accident.

Morgan Hill understood these circumstances but part of his fury was directed at a target beyond Ed Jessup. Hill was fighting memories—seeking revenge against a past he could not forget. He hated the sight of any cabin north of Maverick Creek because it reminded him of the first man who had settled there. In Hill's mind, Ed represented Al Burke, the squatter who had stolen Hill's wife away from him. Now he was protecting his daughter, warning Ed Jessup to stay away.

Regardless of his motives, Hill could not silence Ed as permanently as he had his other dragging victims. Ed had too much at stake. Even if he were destined to be on a lesser scale, Ed wanted the same things Morgan Hill had attained—a place to call his own, a comfortable home he could share some day with a wife and children—children who would inherit their share of this raw and demanding land, and be able to walk with pride upon the rolling Texas prairie. Only the Triple J promised him such a future, and Ed did not intend to abandon his heritage.

His pain-fogged mind could not shut out the echo of the Skillet owner's warning: "You can't stay. Get out by Thursday at noon."

That was only two days away, and Ed knew he would not rest easy during that time. He had no idea what would happen when the deadline arrived, but he knew he would not run—not as long as he could stand on his feet and lift a gun.

Chapter Four

When Ed got home the Triple J cabin was dark and silent. He rode slowly into the ranch yard and turned toward the nearest corral, dreading the chore of unsaddling the horse. There was no moon, but the starlight put a silvery sheen on the sweat which coated his bare chest.

Five miles beyond the cabin, Mescalero Ridge loomed upward like the prow of a gigantic black ship, marking the northern boundary of the Triple J graze. Strangely, perhaps guided by the threat which hung over the Triple J now, Ed's thoughts turned back to the day they had hauled his mother's coffin to the top of the ridge by wagon. They had placed her in a grave among the stunted cedars and pines because his father had said he did not want her where cattle would tramp across her. She had died thinking of Morgan Hill as a friend, Ed recalled bitterly.

Fighting pain, Ed unharnessed the buckskin and turned it free. Aroused by the activity, the other horses in the corral began to mill about, trotting around the pole fence and whinnying in alarm, but the noise did not awaken his father. He slipped inside the cabin and heard John Jessup's spasmodic snoring coming from the rear part of the house.

In his own bedroom, across the narrow hallway from his father's, Ed shucked off the rest of his tattered clothes and lay down on the covers of his bed. Sleep was impossible. Every time he moved, the bed felt like it was filled with a thousand needles, all of them pricking at the raw places on his skin.

The pain not only tortured his body, but also fired his mind with hate. He wanted to get even with Morgan Hill and hurt the arrogant rancher as badly as he had been hurt—but how? The most satisfying way, he thought, would be to kill him. He visualized the two of them standing face to face, legs braced, hands hovering above their six-guns. Morgan Hill was not good with a handgun, but Ed was. He would yell out a warning and give him a head start, then he would put a bullet between those granite gray eyes.

Ed shifted his weight cautiously in the bed and stared at the dark ceiling. He had to stop imagining things that were not likely to happen, he told himself, and concentrate on reality. If Morgan Hill fulfilled his threat to run them off of Maverick Creek, he would not come alone. He would bring the whole Skillet crew.

There was nothing he could do about their predicament tonight, Ed knew, and he wanted to forget about things yet to come. He needed sleep to soothe both his body and his mind, but no matter what position he tried, his worries and the pain in his torn flesh kept him awake.

Around three o'clock, he got up, slipped on a clean pair of Levi's, and hobbled into the kitchen. He rummaged through the cupboard until he found a bottle of whiskey, then carried it, along with a glass, to the square table in the center of the room. He eased himself into a chair, hoping a few drinks would numb his pain and allow him to rest.

He had taken only a sip of the whiskey when John Jessup appeared in the doorway, blinking his eyes and buckling his belt around the Levi's he had pulled on over his red flannels. His father stood still a moment, adjusting his eyes to the lamplight; then his mouth fell open beneath the sweeping white mustache, and he took a quick step toward the table.

"Damn!" John Jessup breathed. "What happened to you, son? Looks like you've been mauled by a cougar."

"Worse," said Ed. "I've been dragged on a rope by a couple of Skillet men, and Morgan Hill was there giving the orders."

John Jessup paced around the chair, sucking in his breath and swearing softly while he surveyed his son's torn flesh. He put a knobby hand on top of Ed's head, tilting it so the lamplight could wash across his son's face. There was a lumpy bruise over Ed's left eye, a cut across the bridge of his nose, and a blood-crusted gash which ran all the way across his chin.

"Damn!" John Jessup swore again. "I heard you clattering around in here. I thought you must be hungry. I didn't expect anything like this. I'd better try to doctor you up some. You're tore up pretty bad, Ed."

With alcohol and turpentine, John Jessup swabbed out the cuts and slashes, occasionally showing Ed the dirt and grime which had remained lodged in the skin despite his bath in the creek. Afterward, he coated the wounds with a sweet-smelling ointment which came from a shiny black tin with a brilliant red rose printed on the side of it. John Jessup had bought a half dozen cans of the salve at a traveling medicine show years ago, and it had proven remarkably effective against burns, cuts, and insect bites.

While his father worked, Ed told him of his failure to buy the Herefords, of his trouble at the stage station, and how Morgan Hill had followed him out on the prairie and ordered him dragged. The story came out in gasps and grunts as Ed paused at times to grit his teeth against the burning of alcohol and turpentine. His father finally put the medicines aside and sat down in a chair across the table from him.

Ed took a drink of the whiskey and looked across at his father. John Jessup's once full face was now shrunken and drawn by age, the points of his cheeks sharp and bony. His narrow eyes, pale blue like those of his son, were dull and listless. The handlebar mustache looked oversized above his sharp chin. The long-fingered hands, once so swift with a gun that his name was known throughout the West, were now stiff with rheumatism.

Ed sipped at the whiskey and waited for his father to comment on Morgan Hill's threat against the Triple J, but since he had finished treating his son's wounds he had said nothing. Ed was not sure the seriousness of their situation had registered in John Jessup's mind.

"He's ordered us to pull out in two days, Pa," Ed said. "He wants to leave some money at the bank and be rid of us forever. We're going to have to fight him, Pa."

John Jessup's head bobbed up and down, but his eyes remained focused on the wall beyond Ed's back. "They cut off Bear River Tom's head, you know. Chopped it off with an ax right down to his shoulders."

"What are you talking about, Pa?"

"Bear River Tom Smith," John Jessup said. "Marshal up in Abilene at the time. Happened nine or ten years ago, back in seventy, I think it was. Tom went out to bring in some farmer who was mixed up in a killin', and he got waylaid in the dark. Somebody come at him with an ax and chopped off his head. That's when they brought in Bill Hickock. I could have had that job. They sent me a letter and wanted

42

me to come up and talk, but I didn't go, so they hired Wild Bill. Maybe I should have gone, but your ma was against it."

Ed gave his father a stony stare, and he felt a tight lump in his throat. It was hard to get used to the fact that John Jessup sometimes had trouble keeping to reality. As soon as he sat down at the table his mind started rambling on some old trail, tracking back through the past which he so frequently confused with the present.

Ed wondered how much help his father would be if it came to a fight with Skillet. There had been a time when Morgan Hill would not have dared challenge Jericho John Jessup, but those days were gone, Ed knew, wrapped up in the yellowed newspaper clippings which were stored in an old leather trunk in the tool shed. Ed had read those clippings since childhood, remembering best the one which had given Jericho John his famous nickname.

It had happened in Cheyenne, when John Jessup was a deputy U.S. Marshal for Wyoming Territory. In reporting a gunfight involving the marshal, the reporter had found it necessary to distinguish between two men with the same name to avoid embarrassing a local resident. The writer had made no attempt to disguise his personal feelings, and Ed could remember the account almost word for word.

Word has come to us, the story began, *that wagging tongues among those who patronize the saloons and brothels of our fair city have expressed dismay over the false rumor that the Rev. John Jessup, respected pastor of the Baptist Church, shot a man to death on the streets of Cheyenne last Monday. As usual those drink-hazy minds are not aware of the facts.*

The man was gunned down by a U.S. Marshal, and his deed might be considered a gift of charity as beneficial to mankind as those frequently dispensed by our good reverend, al-

though he was nowhere near the scene. The marshal's name truly is John Jessup, lately of Jericho Wells, Texas, and to prevent further confusion and falsehoods we shall refer to him as "Jericho John" and present to our readers an accurate account of the incident.

They met on the back side of town, two rawhide-tough men whose characters have been shaped in different molds by the turbulent western frontier. One was a notorious rustler and ambushing killer, the other a man dedicated to protecting the lives and property of decent citizens in a land where outlaws and ruffians outnumber badges of authority by an overwhelming margin.

It was said that Frank Dawson had been seen on the streets of Cheyenne for several days before Marshal Jericho John Jessup spotted him entering a house reportedly occupied by an acquaintance of the wanted man. There under the midday sun, the marshal called the killer out and informed him he was under arrest for a number of crimes. A gunfight erupted shortly thereafter and witnesses recounted for this writer the cool demeanor and exceptional skill of the daring lawman who is making only a brief stopover in our town.

The outlaw put up a bold front, boasting he had outshot a dozen fast guns in his time, and declared he meant to kill the lawman on the spot rather than surrender. Jericho John was undaunted. He told the killer to make his choice — either to jail or to the undertaker.

When Dawson went for his gun, the marshal seemed to move hardly a muscle, but a Colt pistol suddenly appeared in each hand. He shot Frank Dawson dead in his tracks before the outlaw could fire a shot. Hardcases such as Frank Dawson are not welcome in these environs, but Jericho John Jessup will find a most hearty welcome any time.

Other clippings told of the smoky years of John Jessup's career. Newspapers seized upon the eye-catching nickname and kept track of his exploits: JERICO JOHN CAPTURES CUTTER BROTHERS, WOUNDS ONE . . . BANK

His services brought premium pay, and John Jessup
had moved from job to job. He served as a deputy
sheriff in Nueces, town marshal at Cold Springs, and
worked as a Pinkerton man for a while. Banks and
stage lines posted rewards for those who victimized
them, and John Jessup collected bounty after bounty.
He had a growing son, a young wife, and age was
creeping up on him, but John Jessup had planned for
the future. During those hectic years, he saved his reward money, and with it he finally bought the land
along Maverick Creek.

Until he was nine years old, Ed Jessup had lived in
hotels, boardinghouses, and the back rooms of pioneer
jails. The day they moved to Maverick Creek to settle
on a place of their own was the happiest time Ed and
his mother had ever known.

His mother had not lived long enough to enjoy the
life she had dreamed about, however. She had been
struck down by pneumonia four years later. Now all
the hopes Ed Jessup had kept alive in her memory
were about to be wiped out by Morgan Hill's venge-
ance.

"What do you think, Pa?" Ed asked as the silence
dragged on in the kitchen.

"About what?"

"Morgan Hill," Ed said impatiently. "His order for
us to pack up and get out."

John Jessup rubbed a hand through his thinning
gray hair, his eyes again alive and alert. "Don't worry
about it, son. You ain't exactly been mixed up in a
pitched battle. What you and Morgan went through
in town, and out on the prairie, was something of a
difficulty — settling a grudge. Morgan will ponder it
overnight and let it pass at that."

Ed drained the last of the whiskey from the glass. "It's more than that this time. It's more like a war. He wants Molly to marry into a rich family, and he wants me out of her sight, and he wants this land. He's been holding back, thinking of our place like money in the bank to be cashed in when he needs it. He's going to take it if he can, Pa."

"No, son." A smile lifted the ends of John Jessup's mustache. "Morgan won't bother me. That would be an insult to his nature, somethin' as bad as spittin' on his mother's grave. Morgan says those of us who came out here early to tame this country down for civilization will be in more history books than all the generals of the Civil War. Morgan sets a store by history, you know. He wants to be a part of it. That's why he tags around after everybody who's earned a rep, 'specially a gun rep.

"He was tellin' me one time about a trip he took all the way to Abilene back in seventy just to shake Wild Bill's hand. He claims he run into John Wesley Hardin up there. Imagine braggin' about meetin' a killer like that. About that time Wes Hardin had already killed seven men, and he wasn't even twenty years old. Hell, Morgan is still talkin' about that scrap at the Alamo when Colonel Travis and Jim Bowie and Davy Crockett got wiped out by the Mexicans."

Pausing, John Jessup looked at the scowl on Ed's face and chuckled. "It's hard to believe, but Morgan calls me a livin' legend. I've heard him brag out loud to folks about knowin' me. No, son, Morgan won't push me too hard. He's afraid folks might look down on him if he used his power to crowd out a livin' legend."

Ed shook his head sadly. "He's going to push, Pa. I could see it in his face. He figures you've made all the history you're going to make, and he's going to push."

"I guess Morgan's right about my rep," his father said softly. "There's somethin' I never told you about that, Ed. When I moved here I'd already lost more than my hankerin' to go on ridin' for the law. I'd lost my nerve. It got so every time I—"

"You want a drink, Pa?" Ed interrupted. He fidgeted uncomfortably in his chair, not wanting to hear any more. But John Jessup declined the offer with a wave of his hand and continued.

"It got so I had nightmares about bullets hittin' me in the mouth, and I'd dream about blood gushin' out of me. There was a lot of fast guns wantin' to challenge me—gun-crazy kids who wanted to be known as the man who gunned down Jericho John. Every time I rode a strange trail or walked down a street in daylight, sweat was breakin' out on me and my hands were shakin'. Your ma had always wanted me to take up ranchin', so I did, but my nerve was gone. That's why I walked soft around Skillet. I never wanted to fight Morgan Hill man to man."

Ed dropped his glance to the red-and-white checked tablecloth, not wanting to look at his father. While he spoke, Jerico John's gaunt face had gone slack.

Ed said, "I guessed a long time ago that something like that was bothering you, Pa, but it's nothing to be ashamed of. You did your part to make it safe for folks to live a decent life in this country, and you retired. You don't have to do a thing now that you don't want to do. If you want to take Morgan Hill's money and pull out, that's what we'll do. You could live out your life on what you'd get, and I can always get a riding job somewhere that—"

"Never!" John Jessup cut in. "This place has been the best part of your life, and I know you're countin' on it for your future. With some hard work you could be a wealthy man some day. Your ma wanted that for all of us, and I won't take it away from you. I don't have the guts anymore to go eye to eye with a man, knowin' I could die in a split second if my hand is too slow, but I won't run, Ed. I'm still mighty handy with a Colt if I don't have to try to beat somebody's draw, and nobody can outshoot me with a rifle. We'll fight if we have to, son."

John Jessup rose, flexing his stiff knees slowly as he forced himself to stand tall. There was a stubborn tilt to his chin, and a hard glint in his eyes. "Let's get some rest, Ed, and don't worry so much. Morgan was just blowin' smoke. You'll see."

Ed stayed at the table until his father had gone down the hallway to his bedroom The whiskey had warmed his belly, and some of the pain in his body had subsided. He rose, blew out the lighted lamp which he had placed on a shelf above the stove, and went to his own room. For a while he lay wide-eyed on the bed, wondering if his father felt as much confidence as he had expressed. Ed did not, and the knot of dread in his stomach was still there.

Chapter Five

At daybreak Ed was up again, awakened by the sounds of his father puttering around in the kitchen. He went outside, drew a pan of water from the pump at the back corner of the house, and splashed it over his face and neck. He had slept soundly for about three hours, and, despite the soreness of his skin, he now felt fairly strong.

When he joined his father in the kitchen, John Jessup eyed him skeptically. "You ought to stay in bed today, Ed. Some of them cuts look bad."

"We've got too much work to do, Pa. Skillet has probably gathered a thousand cows by now, and we haven't even started. I think I can ride all right."

John Jessup put bacon, beans, and a big platter of hot biscuits on the table. "If we rounded up everything we have it wouldn't be more than three hundred head. That's about the way it works out every year. We sell off about a hundred a year, wait for the calf crop, and then we're about back where we started. The money pays off our winter debts, gets us a couple pairs of Levi's and a shirt apiece, and that's about it. Sometimes we can bank forty or fifty dollars, but I guess I ain't done much with this place. I've just marked time."

"We'll do better, Pa. We've got a little money ahead, so we'll just sell fifty or sixty head this year, let the herd build some, and we'll brand more calves. We've been too careful about that."

A worried look settled across John Jessup's face. He looked sternly at his son. "Don't get any notions about Skillet calves, Ed. I don't want no arguments with Morgan Hill."

Ed stiffened. "Are you forgetting what happened yesterday? We've already got an argument with Hill."

"I've been thinkin' on that," his father said. "I can't figure whether Hill is just hell-bent to keep you away from Molly, or whether it's the land he's after. I understand some of his aggravation. He's done a lot of hurtin' over his wife. You know what happened to her, don't you?"

Ed sighed wearily. "I've heard that story a hundred times, but I don't aim to be punished for what another man did."

The curt tone of Ed's voice caused his father to grow silent and busy himself with his food.

Ed's enthusiasm for the roundup was stronger than it had been in years. He had missed the opportunity to buy the Herefords and improve the quality of the herd, but eventually he would find some. In the meantime, he meant to be more aggressive than before, scouring the brush and arroyos for animals that might have been overlooked. He would make a complete tally this year, counting every head of livestock the Jessups owned instead of making rough estimates, and he would sell only the fattest steers, those which would bring top prices, holding back more good breeding stock than had been the practice in the past.

These were the things they discussed as they rode the Triple J range, and Ed could see that his father was pleased by his renewed interest in the ranch. For the next few hours Ed forgot about Morgan Hill and lost himself in his work, but the first calf they started to brand brought an argument from his father.

Ed roped the yearling and led it up close to the small fire where his father was heating the branding irons. While the horse held the rope, Ed came out of the saddle, threw the calf on its side, and tied its legs with the pigging string he carried clutched between his teeth. While he held the squirming animal on the ground, his father hurried up beside him with the smoking iron in his hand; then John Jessup turned away, swearing.

"That's a Skillet calf, Ed! Turn it loose!"

"The hell it is! There's no mother with it wearing a Skillet brand, and it's been eating our grass. That's good enough for me."

John Jessup spread his legs stubbornly, holding the hot iron away from him. "It's a brindle calf, and its right horn is turned down — that's how I know. Two or three weeks ago it was runnin' with its mother, and she wore a Skillet brand. I guess she weaned it and drifted back across the creek where she belongs. Let it go. I told you at breakfast I don't want to rub Morgan Hill the wrong way."

Sweat rolled off Ed Jessup's bruised face. His lips were tight, his teeth clenched, and he was full of pain. He sprang from the ground, walked to his father, and wrenched the branding iron from the older man's hand. Moving back quickly before the calf had time to start thrashing around, he set his knee against the animal's ribs and pressed the iron against its flank. A wisp of smoke curled into the air, and he turned his face away from the acrid odor of singed hair and hide.

Tossing the branding iron back toward the fire, Ed rose and looked at his father. "It's a Triple J calf now, Pa, and that's the way it's going to be from now on.

Every spring we send a bunch of strays back across Maverick Creek to Skillet just because we think that's where they belong, but they never send any across to us. Morgan Hill doesn't give anybody the benefit of a doubt. His riders put a Skillet brand on every calf they find that doesn't have a branded mother with it."

"It's the same as rustlin'," John Jessup said, "and I purely hate a rustler. That's why I'm after the Cutter brothers. They didn't just steal cows this time. They ambushed two Bar 40 riders; and put four bullets in their backs, but I'll track 'em down. I'll bring 'em in for that."

"You've already done that, Pa," Ed said patiently. "You put the Cutter brothers away twenty years ago. We're working our own cattle now. Let's get back to it. We're not stealing anything. It's got nothing to do with the Cutter brothers."

John Jessup peered intently at his son for a few seconds, then dropped his gaze to the ground. A flush crept over his face as he realized his mind had been wandering. "Hell, son, I was just joshin' about the Cutters. I know they're gone. I'll go along with you on the calf. Folks have been brandin' mavericks for years. What's fair for the goose is fair for the gander, as they say."

Still looking slightly abashed, John Jessup went to his horse and rode off through the sage clumps in search of more calves. Ed did not follow him immediately. He stood a while bent at the waist, his hands resting on his knees while he cursed the agony his exertion was bringing to his lacerated back and chest. Finally, he pulled himself aboard his horse and followed the path taken by his father, but he knew most of his stamina was spent.

Ed had thought he could make it through the day, but he had to give up about noon and return to the ranch house. His father went with him, and for most of the afternoon he hovered over Ed's bed. The old man again cleaned and treated Ed's wounds. Some of the deeper cuts were swollen, and fluid oozed from them.

By dusk, Ed felt better, and he ate a hearty supper. They turned in early, but Ed slept fitfully. His father did not rest much better. Ed heard him get up and down several times, making trips to the outside privy, and then pacing around his bedroom. Morgan Hill's deadline was only a day away, and Ed knew his father was as uneasy as he was. Despite his show of confidence, John Jessup was not at all sure the Skillet owner still maintained the peculiar hero-worship he had once evidenced toward the name of Jericho John.

At breakfast, they talked only of range work, neither of them speaking of the real worry which lurked at the back of their minds. His father tried to persuade Ed to stay in the cabin for the day rather than risk aggravating his injuries further, but Ed waved the idea aside, and at dawn they rode out together.

Had Ed known it was the day he would run into Brady Wayne, he might have accepted his father's suggestion. He had grown so accustomed to the throbbing aches in his body that he worked faster than he had the day before. By midmorning, he and his father had put together a bunch of twelve fat steers. John Jessup stayed behind while Ed started pushing the first bunch toward the flatlands along Maverick Creek where they would establish the holding grounds for the cattle they wanted to sell. A few at a time, they would herd other steers into the area, and group them again in about three weeks when a cattle broker would come by to make a deal.

When the steers were in place, he rode on to the edge of the stream to water his horse. Ed was readjusting the bridle, getting ready to ride back and join his father, when he saw the horseman through a break in the cottonwoods on the opposite side of the creek. The gurgling of water rushing over the rocks had drowned out the sound of hoofbeats, and Ed was somewhat startled to see the man there.

It was Brady Wayne. Wayne sat with his hands folded on the pommel, staring across at Ed. The Skillet foreman had swapped his big white "town hat" for an old black Stetson with a broken brim that flopped down. Despite his boyish face, there was nothing soft and gentle about Brady Wayne. He was as tall as Ed, just a shade under six feet, and he was hard muscled and tough. His walk was arrogant, but he sat in a saddle with the easy grace of a Comanche brave.

"What do you want here, Wayne?" Ed called as the man continued to stare at him.

Brady Wayne drew his right hand back to his belt buckle where it was closer to the holstered Colt on his right leg. "I was on my way up to your place to see if you've got your household plunder packed on a wagon yet. Morgan sent me into Singletree yesterday with instructions to the bank. The money is all set up for you, and the papers are there. Morgan will sell your herd at market price, and send that money on, too. He said to tell you that."

With a snap of the reins, Brady Wayne started his horse across the creek toward Ed. They were less than thirty feet apart. Ed could see the sparkle of the Skillet foreman's even white teeth as the man smiled for no reason.

"Don't come on our land!" Ed said. The sharpness of his voice made Wayne pull the horse to a halt. "This is between the Jessups and Morgan Hill, Wayne. Don't get mixed up in it."

A dry laugh rattled in Wayne's throat. "Morgan has

got twenty cowhands on his payroll and four more men who look after the hay crop. A man like Hill doesn't do his own errands — he hires people to do them. I get paid for things like this, so I'm already mixed up in it."

"What about the others farther up the creek — Sam Ditmar, Harve Grayson, Matt Latham?"

"Don't worry about them," Wayne said. "Just worry about yourself. You've got until noon tomorrow to get away from Maverick Creek. Morgan told me to see to it, and I aim to do just that."

A wave of dizziness blurred Ed's vision for a moment. It was the second time he had experienced such a feeling in the last hour. It was forced away by the anger which surged through him, and he swung into the saddle, keeping his eyes on Brady Wayne.

"We're not going anywhere, Wayne. That's a message you can carry to Morgan Hill. I'll never leave the Triple J as long as I'm alive."

The smile left the Skillet man's face. He straightened stiffly, rippling the long yellow hair which fell around his shoulders. "Then you might go dead," he said grimly. "You sure as hell might go dead."

Ed did not reply to Wayne's threat. He turned the buckskin around and sent it slow-walking away from the creek, leaving Brady Wayne to stare at his back. When he had gone less than a mile, he saw his horse's ears prick up alertly, and then he heard the thud of hoofbeats behind him. Twisting in the saddle, he looked along his back-trail, his nerves tingling. Moments before he had crossed over a small rise, and the swell of the land kept him from seeing who was following him.

A shiver ran down Ed's spine. He looked around for cover, wondering if Wayne had decided to make his fight now. He guided his horse behind a screen of gnarled mesquite trees which grew in a cluster a few yards to his left and slid to the ground, holding one hand over the horse's muzzle to keep it quiet while he lifted his gun free of the holster with the other.

He waited, peering through the trees at his back-trail until the rider came into view; then he put the gun away and stepped into the open. Coming toward him aboard a sleek pinto was Molly Hill.

Her horse was moving at a brisk trot, and she did not try to slow its pace until she was almost in front of Ed. The horse fought against the unexpected bite of the bit, ducked its head, and nearly unseated the girl before she could grab the saddle horn and hold on. Although she had spent her life in ranch country, Molly had never learned to ride well. She almost fell when she failed to kick free of the stirrup as she started to step to the ground. Instinctively, Ed jumped forward to grab her waist, and afterward, he was not sure Molly's clumsiness was as accidental as it seemed.

While his hands rested lightly on each side of her waist, Molly dropped the pinto's reins and whirled so that Ed's arms encircled her. She was dressed in Levi's and a baggy flannel shirt which bloused around her slender waist. He felt the softness of her full breasts pressing against his chest as she hugged him.

Ed pulled away from her, his face puzzled, his gaze sweeping over the prairie behind her. "Why did you come here, Molly? You ought to know better."

"I needed to see you," she said. Her cool green eyes searched his face, and she ran her fingers gently over the bruise above his left eye. "They didn't tell me what they did to you."

"It's not exactly the kind of thing people like to talk about."

Molly drew her hands away from him and clasped them together in front of her waist. "I learned just this

56

morning how they dragged you. I found out then only because I was eavesdropping on a conversation between Brady Wayne and my father. They were wondering if you were laid up in bed, and said maybe you wouldn't be able to pull out by noon tomorrow like my father ordered you to."

"So you know about that, too?"

"Yes. After Brady left the house, I made Dad tell me all about it. I tried to talk him out of it, but he wouldn't listen. I also heard him tell Brady to ride up here and check on you, so I followed him. While the two of you talked I was hiding in the cottonwoods downstream. I couldn't hear, but I can guess what Brady had to say. Brady likes to be in charge of things. After you rode off, he headed toward Comanche Draw where the Skillet crew is working, and I came on to catch up with you."

Ed sighed, irritation showing in his eyes. "Sneaking around like this is a good way to make things worse than they are. You shouldn't have come here, Molly. Somebody from Skillet might be watching us right now. If Morgan Hill hears we've been together, he'll kill me—or have me killed. You saw what happened in town."

"Yes," Molly said softly. She ran the tip of her tongue along her lips and looked at him from eyes hooded by long lashes. "You were wonderful, Ed. So—so dominating the way you slapped Brady around and then beat him to the draw. He thinks he's tough, but you were fast and mean, Ed. Now he knows what a real man looks like."

Ed frowned. The excitement in her voice and her flushed cheeks and dreamy eyes reminded him of the expression he had seen on her face during the fight at the stage station, and he did not like it. "You must enjoy seeing a man put his life on the line. Somebody

57

could have been killed that day. It's not a game, Molly."

Sensing his disapproval, Molly lifted her chin and looked away, her lips fixed in a girlish pout. "Well, watching two strong men go at each other sure beats anything I saw in St. Louis. The young men there talk about nothing but banks, railroads, and which restaurant serves the finest food. They're boring and stupid!"

Her mood changed abruptly. When she looked again at Ed, one eyebrow slightly arched, she was smiling. "Texas grows real men, and I like that. They know what they want, and they know they have to fight to get it. I still think the way you handled yourself in Singletree was wonderful."

"All it got me was a pack of trouble."

"We can put an end to the trouble," Molly said brightly. "That's why I wanted to see you."

Ed scowled suspiciously. "How can we do that?"

"We can get married," she said. "You know Dad wouldn't run his own son-in-law out of the country. People would talk. Don't you see, Ed? It's as simple as that. We can live at Skillet. One day we'll own Skillet. We can get married today. All we have to do is stay out of Singletree where someone might spot us and send word to Skillet. We can ride over to Mesa Springs and find a preacher. If we leave right now, we can be married by sundown."

Molly's words tumbled one upon the other as the plan expanded in her mind. She edged closer to him, her face tilted upward, her hands reaching out for him.

Ed put his hands on her shoulders and held her at arm's length. He was not certain how he should react to her proposal. Either Molly had changed a great deal in the past year, or he had never known her as well as he thought he did. Her unusual fascination

58

with violence and the threat of explosive events disturbed him. He was ashamed of the thought, but he was not sure she did not actually create trouble simply to experience the thrill of being a part of it.

"I always thought you would want to marry me," Molly said. There was a nervous tremor in her voice.

"Maybe someday, but we haven't seen each other for a long time, Molly. We need time together to talk and be sure we still feel the same. I'd never marry you just to get my hands on a part of Skillet or to get your old man off my back. That's a coward's way out, and I'd spend the rest of my life being ashamed of it, and so would you. Maybe we can spend some time together when this thing is over."

"You may not be around when this is over," Molly said.

Ed shrugged soberly. "Maybe not. We'll just have to wait and see."

Forcing his arms apart, she moved against him. She slipped her arms around his waist and pulled his body hungrily against hers. "Make love to me, Ed. We're alone and nobody can see through the mesquite trees. Make love to me so I'll always remember it. Let's do it, Ed. Please!"

Ed pulled away from her, wincing as her hands scraped across the raw places on his back. "Go home, Molly," he said gently. You're going to get me killed if you don't. I don't want to make things worse until I find out what's going to happen tomorrow. Morgan Hill would go loco if he heard we've been together. Go home, Molly."

A faint, sobbing gasp escaped Molly's lips. She turned on her heel and started hastily toward her horse, then she stopped and turned with her hands on her hips. Her eyes were narrow and angry.

"Do you want me to marry Brady Wayne, Ed? Is

that what you want?"

"Why do you ask me something like that?"

Molly smiled smugly. "Because that's what my father wants. He's been pushing us together ever since Brady came to work at Skillet. Dad has told me a dozen times how pleased he'd be if Brady and I could make a go of it."

"What does he find so special about Brady Wayne?"

She continued to smile, seeing the worry in Ed's face and enjoying it. "Brady is more than just another drifting cowhand. He's the son of Roscoe Wayne, who owns the Snaketrack Ranch down near the Pedernales River. Snaketrack is almost as big as Skillet, and Dad would like to see it come into the family. He wants to be the biggest cattleman in the West. It's an obsession with him. If I marry Brady, he thinks he can talk Roscoe Wayne into merging the two spreads, put both under the Skillet brand. Then he wants to pool their money and buy another ranch in Colorado. He says he'd call the ranches Skillet I, Skillet II, and Skillet III."

Ed let his breath out slowly. "Now I know why your pa has a sudden craving for more land—our land—and why he wants me out of your sight. It looks like a lot of high-powered scheming has been going on at Skillet."

He gathered up his horse's reins and stepped into the saddle. Over his shoulder, he said, "My pa is waiting back in the sage for me. He's going to get worried and come looking for me if I don't show up."

"I asked you a question," Molly shouted at him. "Do you want me to marry Brady Wayne?"

"You'll have to make up your own mind about that, Molly. You'll have to decide whether you want to marry a cattle brand or a man."

"That's what I'm thinking about right now," she said.

"Maybe you're not the man I thought you were. Brady Wayne wouldn't push me away. Maybe he's the only real man on this range."

"Maybe he is," Ed said, and sent his horse galloping away without looking back.

Chapter Six

They moved silently around the cabin the next morning, talking little. Neither Ed nor his father ate much breakfast. After cleaning up the dishes, they headed out to the range shortly after dawn, determined to start this day as they did all the others, but both were keenly aware of the uncertainty which lay ahead of them. Morgan Hill's deadline was at noon.

They had worked until dusk the day before, but their hearts were not in the effort, and they did not accomplish a great deal. By the time Ed had returned in late afternoon to the place where he had left his father while he drove the steers to Maverick Creek, John Jessup had branded only two calves. Ed had found him sitting on an outcropping of rock, staring vacantly into space, mumbling to himself.

Afterward, they had spent their time riding in and out of the brush and arroyos, spotting bunches of mature steers they planned to offer the cattle broker. Ed had told his father of his meeting with Brady Wayne, but the old man had shrugged the incident aside. He insisted that Brady Wayne's behavior was just bluff. He was sure Morgan Hill would not violate their long friendship. Ed shook his head, frustrated. He could not convince Jericho John that Morgan Hill was no longer a friend.

Feeling it was too personal to discuss, Ed had said nothing of his encounter with Molly Hill, but he could not put the girl out of his mind.

During the night he had lain awake a long time thinking of the times he had held her in his arms, never wanting those moments to end. Those memories seemed distant and unreal. Molly had changed. He was no longer sure of his feelings toward her, but his sleep was disturbed by a sense of guilt. He should have expressed some gratitude for her efforts to help him escape her father's wrath.

The tension of counting down the hours to Morgan Hill's deadline, combined with the long hours in the April sun, had drained their energy. Ed and his father had gone to bed as soon as supper was finished. After he finally put thoughts of Molly out of his mind, Ed slept soundly for a while, but he awoke some time in the early morning hours with his teeth chattering and chills shaking his bones.

A few of the cuts on his back were beginning to fester, and when he had undressed, Ed noticed the angry red lines which surrounded the wounds. He was not surprised he had developed a fever, but it worried him. He needed to be well and alert by noon. When it was time to get up, he found himself and the covers soaked with perspiration, but the chills were gone.

Overnight, a change had taken place in John Jessup. As he walked toward the corral where Ed waited with two saddled horses, he carried himself a little more erect, his rawboned shoulders squared. His battered brown Stetson was pushed back on his head, and there was a fierce gleam in his pale eyes. Ed had not seen his father wear a gun in years, but today he had strapped on his set of matched Colts, the oiled holsters tied down midway along his thighs. The guns looked freshly cleaned. The cedar butts were worn smooth and dark from years of use.

"That's a lot of weight to pack around, Pa," Ed said, eyeing the guns.

John Jessup swung into the saddle of his roan. "I've always worn two guns when I wore any. They give you good balance when you're afoot. Even if you don't use 'em both at once, you've got a spare when one jams or runs empty. That's saved my hide more than a time or two."

He excused the weight of the guns, but he did not say why he had chosen to wear them. An explanation was not necessary. He was aware that Morgan Hill's deadline was only a few hours away, and, despite his denials, John Jessup was expecting a fight. From the glow in his cheeks, and the keyed-up energy of his movements, it appeared he was even looking forward to it.

They worked around the foot of Mescalero Ridge, chasing out steers in twos and threes until they had put together a bunch of twenty cows. Afterward, they drove them south a few miles, finally herding the longhorns into a wide, grass-grown coulee where they would stay put for a few days. From time to time, each of them would glance skyward, marking the path of the sun; then, without a word passing between them, they both turned their horses back toward the cabin.

Only the thud of horses' hooves and an occcasional cawing of a crow broke the silence of the trail. They were too busy with their own thoughts to talk, and there was little that needed to be said.

Ed rode a few paces ahead of his father, his eyes searching the land for any sign of activity. He had clenched his teeth together so long his jaws ached. Every muscle in his body was drawn wire-tight, filling him with a weariness which had not come from work.

It seemed weeks ago that Morgan Hill had sat calmly aboard his black stallion and ordered Ed and Jericho

John Jessup to get out of the country. The waiting and watching was about to end.

As they entered the cabin, John Jessup said, "Maybe we ought to have asked Harve Grayson and Sam Ditmar and Matt Latham to come around today."

Ed gave his father an oblique glance. His father was also afraid, and was wishing for better odds. It was an open admission that he knew a fight with Skillet was coming.

"I didn't want to draw them into it, Pa. It's our problem."

"Maybe, but they moved in here because they figured my rep would make it safe for 'em. They didn't believe Morgan would bother them if he didn't bother me. I feel some responsibility because of that. I still can't believe Morgan is goin' to make any kind of difficulty with me. I just can't."

Ed shrugged. He walked down the hallway to his bedroom, then returned to the front room with a rifle and two boxes of shells. He found a cleaning rod on the mantel above the stone fireplace, and shoved an oily cloth through the rifle barrel with it, even though he had cleaned the gun only a week ago.

While he filled the rifle with cartridges, Ed looked around the room, studying it as though he were seeing it for the first time. The parlor spread across the front of the house, the open beams of the ceiling adding air and space to the room. A few stuffed animal heads hung on the walls and a thick buffalo robe covered the planked floor in front of the horsehair divan. Large leather chairs sat near each of the windows flanking the doorway.

The cabin was not imposing in any way, but it was roomy and comfortable. Ed and his father had managed to keep it almost as clean and orderly as his mother had kept it. Each year they planted a few flowers at each end of the porch, just as she had done that first spring. In the fall, they gathered nuts from the pecan tree she had planted twenty feet beyond the porch. Old-timers in the area had said the tree would never grow there, but it had flourished, spreading in four massive forks and providing shade for the house during the blistering summers. Ed could still feel his mother's love in this house, and he never wanted to give it up.

When John Jessup returned to the parlor, he, too, was carrying a rifle and shells. His shuffling footsteps sounded loud in the stillness as he walked across the room and sat down in the leather chair on the right side of the front door. Tugging the chair around so he could peer through the window, he propped the rifle against the wall, then lifted the twin Colts from their holsters. He spun the cylinders a few times before he laid the guns on the window ledge in front of him.

Ed took up a similar position in the other chair, placing the rifle and extra shells on the floor near his feet.

Heat waves danced above the grass and sage, distorting the horizon as Ed's eyes swept back and forth across the land. The cedar shakes of the cabin roof popped and cracked as the sun climbed to the top of the sky. A hundred yards in front of the house, the prairie fell away in a long slope. Anyone beyond the crest of the rise would be hidden from view. Farther on, level land was visible again, but it was the line between the two areas that held Ed's attention. Between every breath, he expected to see the shape of a horse or a hatted head pop up above the horizon.

The noon hour came and passed. Nothing happened. From the shape of the shadows beneath the pecan tree, Ed knew the sun was no longer directly overhead, but had started its afternoon trek westward. He glanced at the pendulum clock on the mantel. The

66

clock showed a quarter past one.

He looked across at his father. John Jessup sat hunched forward in his chair, still peering intently through the window. Ed rubbed his sweating palms along the seams of his pants and resumed his vigil. They sat that way for another hour, exchanging occasional glances, but saying nothing.

Finally, Ed rose and stretched, trying to relieve the tension in his muscles. A chill ran through his shoulders. He was not sure whether it was the fever returning, or whether the endless waiting was beginning to play tricks with his nerves.

"What do you think, Pa?" Ed asked.

John Jessup stood up and stuffed his guns back in the holsters. "I think I've been right all along. Morgan got hit by a piece of stray lead; it made him mad and he dragged you. He's had time to think things out, and figures he's already evened the score. I think what we ought to do now is catch up on our chores."

"Maybe," Ed said, "but maybe Hill thinks we've already turned tail and run and he doesn't need to check on us. It would be like him to believe there's nobody around who's foolish enough to buck him. I've got a hunch somebody from Skillet has an eye on this place, though. We'll hear from them sooner or later."

The sudden tightening of his lips beneath the sweeping white mustache indicated John Jessup wanted to end the discussion. He walked out of the parlor and into the kitchen. A moment later, the back door rattled as he went out into the yard. Sighing, Ed followed him, but he felt no more at ease than he had since the day he shot the gun out of Brady Wayne's hand and wounded Morgan Hill.

While his father chopped firewood, Ed went to the barn which adjoined the first corral and put some hay out for the horses. Leaning against the fence, he watched idly as the horses flipped hay about with their muzzles, stamping and pawing at it before they started to eat. Later, he and his father puttered around the house, sweeping the floors and brushing at the furniture, straightening things which really did not need to be straightened.

The sun seemed stuck in one spot in the gray-blue sky, and the clock did not want to move its hands. It was the longest afternoon Ed could remember, and the night dragged on just as slowly. He lay awake for hours, his ears straining to catch every sound of the darkened world. All he heard was the chirping of crickets, the far-off wail of a coyote, and the monotonous cry of an owl in the pecan tree near the front porch.

Skillet struck at midnight. The first shot was the flat crack of a rifle, but in the stillness, it sounded like a clap of thunder. Until he sprang erect in bed, Ed was not aware he had been asleep, but his mind did not have to search for reasoning — he was alert at once, and he knew what was happening. The fear and dread which had gripped his nerves for two days were gone now, driven out by the fury which surged through his veins.

He had slept fully clothed, and he came out of bed grabbing for his boots. By the time he had pulled them on, a half dozen more shots had been fired, and he heard the chunk of hot lead burrowing into the cabin walls. The shots were coming from the front of the house.

Ed ran down the hallway to the parlor, carrying his gunbelt and holstered Colt in his hands. He was surprised to find his father already there. John Jessup had raised the window beside one of the leather chairs. He rested a rifle across the ledge and fired methodically.

Powder flashes winked like fireflies along the horizon where the slope dropped away from the Triple J ranch yard. Both pistols and rifles boomed and cracked in the night, one echoing the other as bullets beat against the house like an erratic drumbeat.

"There are a hell of a lot of people out there!" Ed yelled at his father as he ran toward the other window. A slug hummed through the panes just as Ed ducked behind the chair, showering the room with glass. Most of it fell across his back and slid to the floor without piercing his skin. The acrid smell of powder tainted the night air.

"Must be Hoss Ringo and some of his cutthroat bunch," John Jessup said. "I've been expectin' him to show. I had to kill one of his kin over in New Mexico Territory awhile back. Hell, he's kin to everybody, even that Younger crowd, but I never had no truck with the Youngers. They—"

"There's nobody named Hoss Ringo out there, Pa. That's Skillet! They're here to run us out."

His father's voice drifted off in unintelligible mumbles, and Ed snapped off two quick shots at gun flashes he saw in the darkness. At intervals between shots, he listened for voices, trying to identify someone he knew. He could hear horses neighing in fright and an occasional shouted order. But it was so noisy the sounds blended together.

For almost an hour the battle raged on. Ed and his father managed to match one shot for every five or six fired against them. At first the attackers remained out of sight just beyond the crest of the slope. Their shots came in high, striking the upper walls and roof of the ranch house. Little by little, however, they grew bolder, and Ed could see an occasional silhouette along the line which divided the starlit sky from the dark earth.

One rider paused too long against the skyline and Ed held him in his sights and squeezed off a deliberate shot. The pop of the rifle and the man's cry of pain came almost in the same instant.

John Jessup heard the startled voice and chuckled. "That'll learn 'em somethin'. When Morgan finds he's got some buryin' to do, he'll know better than to mess with us Jessups."

Ed's shots were answered by a barrage of bullets, and this time the aim was lower. He dropped to the floor, hearing lead chopping at the window frames and the front door.

Suddenly the firing from outside ceased. A foreboding silence settled over the house, and Ed could hear his own breath hissing in and out. He reloaded the rifle, waited a few seconds, then raised his head cautiously above the window ledge to look outside. He saw no movement. The stillness puzzled him—worried him. He slumped back to the floor. Sweat dripped from his face, and the cuts on his upper body throbbed with pain.

The reason for the lull in the battle was soon apparent. Glass shattered somewhere at the back of the house, and bullets hammered at the kitchen door.

"They've circled us!" John Jessup yelled.

Ed was already moving, feeling his way along the walls to the kitchen. The floor was a mess, speckled with grit and splinters of wood torn from the house. Through a broken window, he saw a powder flash not forty feet away. He fired twice in that direction, but heard no outcry. Rifle and pistol slugs buzzed around the room like a swarm of angry hornets, and Ed hugged the floor for protection. His father called out to him, asking if he was all right. Ed replied reassuringly.

"I'll give you a holler if I get more'n I can handle in here," John Jessup said. His voice was vibrant and forceful. His mind was no longer diverted by memories. He was fighting Skillet, and he knew it. The heat of the battle had pumped him full of energy and enlivened his spirit.

Somewhere near the kitchen wall, Ed heard a voice say, "We're supposed to aim high! Get the windows and the roof! Somebody's shootin' too low! We ain't supposed to kill nobody, just scare 'em out!"

The sound of a moving horse came close, and another voice yelled, "I'm running things here! Just do what you're told!"

There was no need for John Jessup to call when the rush came. Ed heard the pounding hooves and the blowing-wind sound that bunched riders on running horses make in the night. The room was so dark he could barely find his way out of the kitchen, but the silhouette of his father's grim face was outlined clearly against the window.

Suddenly several streaks of flame sailed upward in front of the window, and there was a clatter as firebrands landed on the shingled roof. The earth vibrated outside as horsemen swept around the house. Cracks of light showed along the walls where the continuous barrage of lead had knocked the adobe chinking from between the hewn logs. Some of the bullets were finding their way through the holes, and lead screamed inside the cabin.

John Jessup murmured a curse as a slug knocked glass from the window he had raised above his head.

"You there, Ed?"

"Here, Pa!" Ed dropped to his hands and knees and crawled to his station at the other window. He raised his rifle just in time to get a shot at three riders swinging in a wide circle toward the back of the house.

"I never figured Morgan would turn on me like this," John Jessup growled. "He's been my friend for . . ."

Gunfire drowned out the old man's voice. A slug punched more mud from the wall, sailed through the kitchen doorway, and rang like a bell as it ricocheted off

71

the iron stove. The cedar shingles of the roof were old, curled dry by the summer sun, and they burned like tinder. Already Ed could see patches of flame over his head. Smoke sifted down from the roof like gray fog, and a voice outside shouted, "Tell us when you're ready to ride out, or stay there and burn alive!"

It was an offer to hold fire while they escaped, but Ed was not ready to accept it. He swore under his breath, trying to identify the tone of the voice. It sounded like Brady Wayne, but he could not be sure.

There was no respite in the attack. Again and again the horsemen circled, and more burning torches landed on the cabin roof. John Jessup coughed as the smoke thickened, and Ed blinked tears from his stinging eyes. When the riders came close, John Jessup threw aside his rifle, and his matched Colts blasted away in unison. Long shadows reached out from the cabin walls and the land brightened as the flames on the roof blossomed into a blistering inferno.

The Skillet crew stayed beyond the firelight. Their horses moved in a ragged circle, and Ed and his father fired blindly into the steady hail of bullets.

Somewhere in the darkness a man screamed in pain, and John Jessup let out a cackling laugh. "There's some hot pepper for one, and here comes—"

Ed had been only half listening, but he whirled around as a gun exploded surprisingly close. John Jessup's words stopped abruptly. Still holding his rifle, Ed crawled across the floor, straining to see through the swirling smoke. For the first time, panic clutched at his stomach. He called his father's name, but there was no reply. His hand touched John Jessup's chest and came away sticky.

"I—I'm all right I think," his father said thickly as the shock left him. "Got—me—through a rib, though."

Chapter Seven

His hands shaking, Ed lifted his father to a sitting position. He turned him gently so the growing orange glow outside shone through on the pain-pinched face and blood-splotched shirt. He unbuttoned the shirt and flannel underwear and inspected the wound. The bullet had entered high on the left side and passed all the way through his father's body a few inches below his armpit. There was not much blood around the pulpy red punctures on either side. Ed knew that meant most of it was spilling on the inside.

He sat down hard on the floor beside his father, feeling sick and dizzy. He raised his voice loud enough to be heard above the gunfire and made his terms with the Skillet crew. He asked for time to bind his father's wound, time to gather a few things in two blanket rolls and to saddle the horses. There was silence as the guns outside stopped barking. Only an occasional muted exchange of conversation told him Skillet was still waiting.

There was not much time for packing. Flames were beginning to crawl down the walls of the house, and blazing embers were dropping from the roof to the floor. He left his father propped against the windowsill and hurried down the hallway, blinking his eyes and coughing as he went.

The fire and smoke were not as bad at the rear of the house, and he had time to gather enough to meet their needs for a few days: blankets, tarps, extra shirts, and Levi's from the bedrooms; bacon, coffee, utensils, and a few canned goods from the kitchen. He ran from room to room, putting together two blanket rolls, then hurrying back to his father.

"Don't forget our money," John Jessup said. He had struggled to his feet, bracing himself against a chair, and his voice sounded stronger. "It's in that tin box under my bed."

In his haste, Ed had given no thought to the money he had returned to his father after he had failed to buy the Herefords. It took him only a few seconds to get the bloodstained bills from the metal box and stuff them into a pocket of his Levi's.

They went out the back door, ducking away from the heat which radiated from the cabin walls. Ed carried a blanket roll under each arm, grunting with the weight. His father followed slowly behind him. At the corral, John Jessup insisted he was feeling better, but a glance at his ashen face told Ed his father was putting up a false front. He made him rest against the fence while he brought out their horses, leaving the gate open so the three mustangs left could run free.

From a lean-to next to the barn, Ed picked up a pair of saddlebags and stuffed a hand ax, a Bowie knife, and a few other small tools into the pockets. Among the tools was a short-handled spade which they sometimes used to clean out water holes on the range. Ed tried not to admit to himself why he had brought the shovel, and he wondered if his father would notice it protruding from the saddlebag.

"Better head for Mesa Springs," John Jessup said. "Sheriff Ray Felton's got a sister over there, and I hear tell he stops by to see her once in awhile. Mesa Springs is

74

about the only place he's ever been seen in these parts. Maybe we can find some law and a doctor. We could use the help of both."

The hoarseness of his father's voice sent a shiver along Ed's spine. He said, "That's a long ride, Pa. We can get to Singletree a lot quicker. If we go there, we can get Doc Stratton to patch you up."

"It might not be safe in Singletree. Morgan Hill's got his crew on the rampage, and they won't cool down this day. They've caught mob fever. If any Skillet men show up in town they'll still be lookin' for a fight. . . ." The old man paused and a gagging cough racked his chest. He drew a wheezing breath and continued stubbornly. "We'll do as I say, go to Mesa. We'll mend ourselves some, then we'll come back, if that's what you want."

Ed's jaw tightened. "I'm coming back, Pa. I don't aim to let Morgan have Triple J just for the asking."

He brought the horse close and struggled to help his father into the saddle. They didn't see anyone as they slowly rode away, but a final burst of gunfire sent bullets kicking at their heels.

They fled, an admission of defeat Ed had thought they could avoid, across the rolling prairie and up the slopes of Mescalero Ridge, both weary and wounded. They rested the horses atop the ridge and sat silently in the saddles while they watched the flames far below devour the cabin which had been their home.

John Jessup shook his head feebly. "We were two against a dozen or more down there. Didn't have a chance, and too foolish to know it. That's what happens when you push a man like Morgan Hill."

"Nobody pushed him, Pa. We bowed down to him so long he got the idea we're weak and don't have the guts to fight him. He's always looked at us like we were temporary settlers, holding on until he had a need for the land. When he heard I was trying to build up the Triple J, he

75

figured it was time to get things in order. That shooting scrape in town just gave him an excuse to move against us."

Nodding absently, John Jessup tightened his hand on the saddle horn and rocked his body forward. His face was pale, creased by deep lines, and his arms rested limply on the horse's back. He made an effort to draw himself erect when he saw the anxiety in Ed's face.

"My fault," he murmured. "When I found out Morgan thought I was somethin' special, somebody for the history books, I figured my rep was enough to keep me safe. I just laid low and did mostly what Morgan advised, trying to get by. That put me under his thumb, and I was too stuck on myself to know I was a failure. I can't figure out what made Morgan change. We was friends for a long time, then he got ornery. He's been jumpy for a year or more, complainin' about this and that—complainin' about water bein' scarce, complainin' about you keepin' company with Molly, and—"

Anger flashed in Ed's eyes. "My guess is Brady Wayne had something to do with that. Brady wants to marry Molly and Hill is all for it. They're trying to outdo each other. Brady wants Molly, and he'd like to get his hands on Skillet that way. Hill thinks he'll get his hands on a big ranch Wayne's father owns somewhere on the Perd'nals, but it's more than that. Hill can't forget what happened to his wife, and he hates the sight of anybody who lives on the land the squatter had. And he wants our land. He aims to be the biggest rancher in Texas, if he can. That's how he wants to get in the history books."

John Jessup wiped a horny hand across his eyes, turning his gaze away from the fire destroying his cabin. "We're fightin' a devil of a man, I reckon. I don't see how just the two of us can stop him."

"We'll stop him," Ed said. "We'll stop him if I have to kill off Skillet one man at a time."

Before Ed finished talking, John Jessup started his horse moving again. Ed studied the hunched back and drooping shoulders, and knew he would not be able to count on much help from his father. John Jessup would not be able to fight again for a long time. He was weaving in the saddle, and more and more of his weight rested against the hand he kept propped on the horn.

Through the chill gray hours of dawn, Ed and his father pushed their horses northward toward Mesa Springs. They rode along the crest of Mescalero Ridge, picking their way carefully around brush thickets and stunted cedars. Ed kept his father in front of him, following in silence until he saw a dim yellow glow off to his left, and called the old man's attention to it.

"Sam Ditmar's place!" John Jessup said, reining to a halt. "Skillet's burnin' out Sam, too. Hill's riders have gone plumb wild. They'll move on up Maverick Creek until they get 'em all. Next will be Matt Latham and Harve Grayson, then on to the head of the creek to clean out Clay Siler. By sunup, every man who followed me here will be on the run. They settled here because they thought I was tough enough to make it safe for 'em. Now they're ruined. We're all ruined, and it's my fault."

"Hold on, Pa. You're not burning them out. Skillet's doing that."

"All my fault," John Jessup said again. Ed whirled to face him, hearing sounds that scared him. His father's voice was a gurgling whisper, and there was a froth of blood around his mouth.

"You'd better step down, Pa," Ed tried to sound casual. "You're going to have to rest here while I ride on and try to find a doctor. There's no sense in both of us riding all the way to Mesa."

His father waved him away as Ed tried to move the buckskin closer to him. "All my fault," he repeated. "I—I wanted to live out my days in peace . . . especially after your ma left us. So I . . . acted like I needed Skillet's blessin' to live . . . on land I bought . . . and paid for. But I won't stand . . . for this. Morgan Hill has never . . . never met me face to face with a gun in my—"

He never finished the sentence. Calling on the last of the rawhide toughness which had carried him through a score of gunfights, he had tried to deceive Ed about the seriousness of the wound left by the bullet which had ripped through his insides, but he could not bluff his son any longer. His life had oozed out inside him. His chin dropped heavily on his chest and the reins slipped from his fingers. He pitched sideways from the saddle with very little noise. One boot was still caught in the stirrup.

Before he dismounted to free the twisted foot, Ed knew there was no need to hurry. Jericho John Jessup was dead.

It wasn't much of a burying, but it was the best Ed could do, and somehow it seemed fitting for a man who had lived his life with few comforts and no luxuries. His father had told him many times he never wanted to be hemmed in by a wooden box when his time came. He wanted to be buried with his Levi's and boots on, wrapped only in a tarp so part of his land could be close around him. It was the way most of John Jessup's friends had been laid to rest in the old days, and Ed gave no thought to a coffin.

From the bedroll behind his father's saddle, Ed took a blanket and tarp and wrapped the body. He tied him on his horse and backtracked along the western slope of Mescalero Ridge until he came to the small clearing where his mother was buried.

With the hand ax and short-handled spade, Ed scooped out a grave. He lost account of time, and did not pause to wonder about the mysterious well of strength a

78

man can call upon to do a job that has to be done.

He had to stop and rest about every fifteen minutes, but he kept at the digging, measuring the depth of the grave on his own body — first to his knees, then to his waist, and finally to his shoulders. With cattle ropes, he eased his father's body as gently as possible to the bottom of the pit, keeping his eyes closed as he pushed in the first shovelfuls of dirt. When he had finished, the sun was high in the sky, well past the midday mark, and Ed's clothes were drenched with sweat. He blinked away the tears. Already there was an aching emptiness and a burning fury inside him.

Fatigue sickened his stomach, and his head was filled with buzzing noises. He forced his heavy legs to move him around while he freed the horses to graze, and prepared some cold beans and jerky for himself. Afterward, he stretched out on the ground a few feet from the two earthen mounds among the jack pines, and weariness brought sleep.

A flock of squawking magpies in the scrub pines awakened Ed. He opened his eyes to look up through the darkened trees at a starlit sky. Far-off he could hear the bawling of cattle, and there was a faint smell of wood smoke in the air from the cabins which had been burned miles away on Maverick Creek.

He rose slowly, walking the few yards to his father's grave. For a while he stood staring at it. Tears moistened his eyes and he felt a depressing loneliness. Finally, he moved away, murmuring, "Sorry, Pa."

He picked out the usable items from John Jessup's bedroll and put them with his own belongings, wrapping the rest in a slicker and hiding them, along with the beat-up saddle, in a brush pile. He built a fire and cooked a hot meal, no longer concerned about the Skillet riders. By this time, Morgan Hill would assume his victory was complete. His crew would be busy again with the roundup.

The day's rest had renewed Ed's strength, but his muscles began to quiver as the chills which had bothered him two nights ago started all over again. He felt lightheaded and slightly dizzy, and he knew he was not yet ready to move into the open.

While he ate, his thoughts grew clearer and guilt nagged at him, turning the food tasteless. The events of the past four days seemed almost unreal. He found himself holding his face in his hands, pressing his fingertips against his eyes as though he could push away the memories, but they were still there. His father was dead and every rancher on Maverick Creek had been banished from his land.

He regretted he had not headed directly for Singletree when they fled the burning cabin. It was unlikely, he reasoned, that the Skillet men would have pressed an attack in front of witnesses when there was no visible sign of provocation. They might have reached town in time to save his father. In reality, he admitted, it probably made little difference. From the appearance and location of the wound, Ed had sensed that his father would not live through the night.

He could not restore his father's life, but he could make his death count for something. John Jessup had died defending his land, finally bowing to Ed's determination to rebel against the limitations Morgan Hill had placed on them. Now it was more important than ever that the Triple J be preserved as testimony that John Jessup's efforts were not in vain.

Ed thought of Sam Ditmar, Harve Grayson, Matt Latham, and Clay Siler, wondering what had happened to them. They needed to know that his accidental wounding of Morgan Hill and his casual meeting with Molly were responsible for triggering the raid which had run them off Maverick Creek, and they needed to know he did not intend to surrender to Morgan Hill and that he would fight with them until they regained their land.

He had to fight as long as there was life in him because it was what Jericho John Jessup would expect of him. And he had to do it so he could live with his own conscience.

Sam Ditmar and Harve Grayson had tried to persuade him to stay away from Singletree, and they might feel that the disaster which struck them could have been avoided if he had listened to them. He had to convince them that Morgan Hill's raid was inevitable, regardless of what any of them did.

When he finished his meal, he slipped quietly through the dark brush to the grassy spot where he had left the horses on a picket line. He freed his father's roan, slapped it on the rump and sent it loping down the ridge to the prairie below, where it could fend for itself. Then he reset the line for the buckskin, making sure it could reach the trickling spring which twisted its way off Mescalero Ridge toward the creek below.

He bathed his face in the cool water. His skin was hot and dry, and he quivered with chills. The cold water made his bones ache, but he needed to bring his temperature down if he could. He pulled off his shirt, finding it pasted to his skin with sweat and crusted blood. The cuts began to sting and burn when the water touched them. He washed down to the waist and rinsed out his shirt.

Returning to camp, he found another shirt in his bedroll and left the wet one on a bush to dry. Then he stretched out on the blankets again, worried that his body seemed to need so much rest. It really didn't matter. He needed time anyway to sort out his thoughts and to map a plan which would allow him to hold on to the Triple J and make amends for the trouble he had brought to the others who had lost their holdings on Maverick Creek.

He owed something to Molly, too. He was still somewhat bewildered by her unexpected offer of marriage and by her quick change of mood when she taunted him with a hint that she might marry Brady Wayne instead. She no longer acted like the cheerful, levelheaded girl who had captured his heart years ago. He wanted to see her again in quiet surroundings, and talk earnestly with her and search again for the common interests and affection which had once drawn them together.

Thoughts of her lingered on in his mind before he went to sleep, but he knew it would be a long time before it was safe for him to try to arrange a meeting with Molly — if he would ever see her again. Would she bow to her father's wishes and marry Brady Wayne so Morgan Hill could spread the Skillet brand across Texas and on into Colorado?

In her anger over his rejection, Molly had revealed that such an arrangement was part of Hill's grand scheme to build the biggest spread in Texas, and getting rid of Ed Jessup was the other part. Ed detested the idea of Molly nestling in Brady Wayne's arms, but at the moment, he was more concerned with staying alive.

Chapter Eight

Dawn was sending exploring gray fingers along the eastern sky when Ed stirred in his blankets and swung his glance around the camp. He had slept only at intervals, rising often to keep the fire alive to ease the chills which continued to torment him; but in the last hour before daybreak, he had slept soundly until some subconscious warning disturbed him.

He came instantly awake and reached for the gun which he had placed beneath the saddle he was using for a pillow. Even before he heard the soft thud of a horse's hoof and the whisper of moving pine branches, his inner senses told him he was no longer alone on Mescalero Ridge.

He was up on one knee, the gun extended warily, when the rider broke into view fifty feet away. He sat back down heavily, relaxing all at once when he saw the rider was a girl. She was a small-boned, full-figured girl of about twenty, with ebony black hair pulled back tightly away from her oval face and twisted into a bun at the back of her neck. She had loosened the chin strings on her flat-crowned gray Stetson and let it fall back to rest between her shoulders.

"Don't shoot me, Ed Jessup!" she said quickly. Her dark eyes were large against the creamy tan of her face, and her lips were full and smiling.

"Who're you?"

"You know me — at least you ought to. I've been around most of your life. I'm Ellen Ditmar — Sam's daughter."

She dropped the horse's reins and stepped down with the easy grace of an experienced rider. It was obvious she had done her share of range work on Sam Ditmar's little spread. She wore a plain white blouse and ordinary Levi's, both appearing a size too small. Her thrusting breasts opened small gaps between the buttons of the blouse, and her rounded hips stretched the seams of the Levis.

"I remember you now," Ed said. "I've seen you a few times with Sam, but I guess I didn't pay much attention."

Ellen Ditmar slapped her palm against her leg. "I guess you didn't . . . and you didn't pay me any attention in school, either. I went through all the grades with you and Molly Hill, and I did everything I could to get your attention, but you were too busy lollygagging over Molly all the time. There were times when I thought about taking off my clothes and running naked through the schoolyard to see if you'd notice me. I never liked Molly Hill." She smiled.

Ed stared at her, his interest aroused by this striking, plain-speaking girl. "What have you got against Molly?" he asked.

"She's uppity and sneaky, and gets her enjoys from watching someone else get hurt. She thinks it's real sporty to have people fight over her, and —"

"Were you in Singletree the other day?" Ed cut in. "The day Molly saw me fight Brady Wayne?"

"No. I learned about Molly a long time ago, when we were younger. On days you didn't show up at school, Molly really showed herself. She used to bait the boys just to get them to fight. She'd tell one he could have her

84

if he could catch her, and she'd go running off in the bushes behind the schoolhouse. If the boy caught her and tried to get her clothes off, she'd tell another boy the first one tried to rape her. A fight would break out, and Molly would go off giggling. That was when she was fourteen or fifteen, but I don't figure she's changed much. If I ever tell a man he can have me, he can have me."

Ellen Ditmar had spoken rapidly, her words laced with bitterness. Her voice trailed off, and she shook her head vigorously. "Why am I telling you this?"

"I don't know," Ed said, "but you shouldn't be out here. It's not safe for you to be riding around here after what happened. Why did you come?"

Sadness dulled her almond brown eyes. "I wanted to go back to our place and see if I could salvage anything. We had to get out in a hurry when the fire started, and we didn't save much. I thought the flames might have died out before all my clothes were burned. Last night I couldn't sleep for thinking about it, so I got up early and rode out here, but it was a waste of time. There's nothing left."

"That's pretty risky. Skillet is still working roundup, and you can't tell what their riders have been told to do about the people on Maverick Creek. You shouldn't be riding alone."

Ellen Ditmar shrugged and sat down on the edge of Ed's blanket. "I saw smoke from a campfire up here when I started back, and I guessed it had to be you and Jericho John. I'm not afraid to be alone. There's a rifle in my saddle boot, and I can shoot as good as anybody. Anyway, I doubt if Skillet would bother a girl."

She studied Ed's face closely for the first time. The cuts and bruises had healed, but traces of them were evident in the lighter lines across his tanned face. She said, "We heard about them dragging you. Brady Wayne

85

spread the word around. We thought that was the end of it. We didn't expect to be run out."

Knots of muscle leaped along the edge of Ed's jaw. His pale eyes narrowed. "I guess Brady didn't want to brag about the rest of the deal. Morgan Hill ordered me and Pa to get out, and tried to make it look like a business deal by leaving some money at the Cattleman's Bank for us. He wanted to give us the same as what Pa paid for our place. We refused to run, but maybe we should have. We didn't think he'd bother anybody but us."

His voice softened by sadness, Ed told Ellen Ditmar about the ultimatum issued by Morgan Hill, about the fight at the cabin, the wounding of his father, and of their eventual flight.

When he had finished, the girl's face was pale, but her dark eyes were afire with anger. She glanced around the camp. "How is your father getting along? I've been wondering why I didn't see him around."

"He's dead."

"Oh, my God!" Ellen exclaimed. "And I've been sitting here talking about — about jealousy. I'm sorry, Ed. Can I help? Have — have you buried him?"

"Over there." Ed gestured toward the grave a few yards away, partially hidden by the trees. He pushed to his feet, intending to walk to the graves. The ground rocked beneath him and he lost his balance. He staggered sideways, reaching for the girl's shoulder. She jumped to her feet and grasped him around the waist, but could not support him. Ed slid slowly to his knees and tumbled on his side across the blankets.

Ellen knelt beside him and ran her hands over his face. "You're burning up, Ed. You've got enough fever to kill a horse. I've got to get you to town and see if Doc Stratton can help you. What's wrong with you?"

Shaking his head to clear it, Ed sat up and took a couple of deep breaths. "There are a couple of places on

86

my back which haven't healed right. I've been sort of fading in and out for the last couple of days. I'll be all right directly."

"You must have an infection all through your system," Ellen said. "You're going to die if you don't get help, and we can't have that. We need you. My father and the other ranchers are marking time, waiting to see what Jericho John will do to settle with Skillet. When they hear he's dead they may give up. Pa's already talking about going back to Nebraska, but I'm not going. If nobody else will fight for our land, I'll stay behind and do it myself. I think they'll all stay and fight if they have someone to push them. That's got to be you, Ed."

He nodded as he rested on one knee, then stood up. The girl rose, too, holding firmly to his arm in case he faltered, but the dizziness had passed and his head was clear.

"Where are Sam and the others now? What are they doing?"

"They're all in Singletree except Clay Siler. We heard he's down south trying to trap some mustangs to sell. Everyone is trying to earn their keep, and folks in town have been real nice to us. We've all found something to do. I've got a job in the dining room at the Drover's Pride. I start tomorrow. That gets me room and board, and two dollars a week. Ma is staying with Myrtle Cooper, helping her with her sewing trade to earn her way. There wasn't room for all of us, so Pa and I —" She stopped talking and pushed impatiently at her hair. "I'll tell you about it later. Right now we need to find Doc Stratton and get you fixed up."

"Not today," Ed said as she tugged at his arm. "These spells of mine come and go, and I can hang on awhile. Day before the Skillet raid I was strong enough to work cattle, so I guess I'm better off than I look. You go on back to town and take care of your job. In a couple of days I'll come into Singletree. I want to talk to your pa and the others, but I've got another job to do first."

"You're not going to tackle Morgan Hill by yourself?"

"That's exactly what I aim to do. It might keep us out of a range war."

Ellen Ditmar shook her head. "It might get you killed."

"Your pa and Harve Grayson told me that on the trail the other day, but I'm still around. I take a lot of killing."

Ellen's slim shoulders sagged a little. She turned toward her horse, murmuring, "I hope there isn't any more killing. It's terrible, what happened to your father."

With her hand resting on the saddle horn, she turned and said, "If you're not in town by the day after tomorrow I'm coming back for you . . . and if you put me to all that trouble I don't know what I might do when I get here."

Ed Jessup smiled. It was the first time in more than a week he had felt like laughing. "Are you hinting that you might take off your clothes and run around in the woods naked to get my attention?"

"Even that," she said, returning his smile, "but I'd probably let you catch me."

She dropped her hand away from the saddle and came back to face him. Rising to her tiptoes, she brushed her lips across his mouth in a fleeting kiss, and whispered, "Be careful, Ed!"

A moment later she rode away from Mescalero Ridge, but it was a long time before Ed could stop thinking about her. He had seldom met a woman as outspoken and appealing as Ellen Ditmar. He wondered how he could have given anyone so beautiful such casual notice before. Ellen had admitted that she had been attracted to him since their school days, but he was surprised at the depth of feeling he had seen in her eyes.

Through the rest of the day and night, Ed remained at his remote camp, sleeping on his blankets most of the time. Only once during the night did he feel the recurring chills, but they did not last long, and he slept better than he had the night before.

At sunrise the next morning, he packed his gear and left the ridge. The most direct route to Skillet led across his own land, and Ed turned his buckskin toward home. Two hours later he came into the Triple J ranch yard and rested in the saddle while he surveyed the results of the fire.

Most of the leaves of the big pecan tree were stripped away. Those which remained were curled and wilted and turning brown. The branches nearest the cabin had been burned away, and Ed was not sure the tree would ever live again. It had been like a living memorial to his mother. The sight of it gave him as much reason to hate Skillet as anything else which had happened to him.

The stone chimney stood starkly against the early morning sky like a tall tombstone marking a place of death. A few feet away, warped and broken from the heat, the old iron cookstove was tilted grotesquely on its three remaining legs. Aside from this, there was nothing left of the cabin except a pile of blackened rubble.

A lump grew in Ed's throat and he felt the urge to be away from the place. The outbuildings had escaped the fire, and Ed remained at the ranch long enough to lighten the buckskin's load by stowing his saddlebags in the toolshed near the barn. He turned his horse toward Maverick Creek and the Skillet boundary.

When he reached the creek, he stopped to let his horse drink, and dismounted to stretch his legs. The scent of sage and dew-wet soil drifted around him and birds sang in the cottonwoods which formed a thick screen along the water's edge. There was a sense of solitude and well-being here as he stood upon his own land, but Ed knew the peaceful atmosphere was deceptive.

Proof of this came only minutes after he had climbed

89

aboard the buckskin and found a shallow place to ford the creek. He was just coming out of the fringe of trees on the Skillet side of the creek when he saw his horse's ears prick up, and heard a soft neigh ripple in its throat. He turned quickly to glance at his back-trail, a knot of fear in his stomach.

Ed had looked the wrong way. When he faced forward again, Brady Wayne stepped out from behind a thick patch of brush less than ten yards to Ed's left. The Skillet foreman was leading his horse with one hand and holding a six-gun in the other.

"Step down!" Brady Wayne said sharply.

Ed slid to the ground, careful to keep his hand away from his holster when he saw the wild look in Wayne's eyes.

Dropping his gelding's reins to the ground, the Skillet foreman took three steps forward and stopped again, his heels going down hard in the dirt, his eyes probing Ed Jessup's face. The battered black Stetson was pulled low on his forehead, its broken brim flopping up and down as he walked. His golden face looked soft and delicate, but lumps of muscle quivered along his clenched jaw.

Brady Wayne had been teased for years about his boyish good looks and golden hair. He wore the old hat most of the time, apparently an attempt to look ordinary enough to stop the jokes. It was a mistake, however, for any man to believe Brady Wayne's appearance portrayed a man of mild manners and uncertain nerve.

"I was on my way to check on your place," Wayne said. "I didn't expect to find anybody around, but I'm glad you came along, Jessup."

"You'd better not be so glad about it, Brady." Sight of the man filled Ed with anger. "Skillet killed my pa, and somebody is going to pay for that."

A strange light danced in Wayne's eyes, but it did not change the set of his jaw. "I didn't know Jericho John was dead, but there's no way of knowing who did it. You can't pin it on me. If I was to kill anybody, mister, it would be you. I don't know what Morgan aims to do about you, and I don't care. It's out of his hands now. It's personal between you and me."

"You're just a hired hand, Brady. I figure you were leading that bunch who burned us out and killed my pa, but you can wait. I'm on my way to see Morgan Hill. I'll start with him, and I'll get to you."

Brady Wayne's knuckles whitened against the butt of the Colt. Ed's hand edged a little closer to his own holster. He did not like the wild look on the man's face, and he was afraid Wayne might pull the trigger without giving him a chance to draw.

"You'll start with me, not Morgan," Wayne said. "He pays me to keep people like you away from him, but I'd do it without pay to keep you away from Molly. She's my woman now, but you keep messing around with her. You—"

"I'm not chasing after Molly," Ed said. "She does what she wants to do."

Wayne ignored the interruption. "I saw what happened after you rode away from the creek the other day. Molly figured I'd head straight for Comanche Draw, but I didn't. I saw her come out of the trees and follow you, so I trailed behind. When she caught up to you, I laid down on the edge of the rise and watched. I saw you hugging her and putting your hands all over her. Then you laid her down right there in the mesquite thicket. I thought I heard somebody coming, maybe your pa, and I backed off, but I know you made love to her that day, and I told Morgan you did."

Ed swallowed hard so his voice would not break with anger. "That's a lie," he said softly, realizing at last that the crazed expression in the Skillet foreman's eyes was born of jealousy. "It's a lie, and you know it. Molly is not your woman just because you say she is. She'll decide where she belongs when the time comes."

"She's my woman," Wayne said again. "My old man thinks I'm no good and that I can't make it on my own. But Molly can give me that chance. You're the only person who can ruin that for me. I don't want you around her anymore, and I'm going to show you what it will cost you for trying."

The man's gun hand began to tremble. Ed drew in his breath, his chest tight. "You've got no witnesses here to say there was a fair fight, Brady. You'll be hanged for murder if you gun me down."

Brady Wayne relaxed his grip on the gun. "Maybe, maybe not, but I won't take the chance if you'll do as I say. Otherwise, I'm going to put some lead in you. Now drop your gunbelt. Do it easy, and I'll put my gun down. You're not leaving here without something to remember. I aim to beat the hell out of you with my fists, and I aim to do it every time I see you if that's what it takes to get rid of you. Molly would like that. She likes to see a good fight when she's the prize for the winner."

Eager to get at the man, Ed put his gun on the ground immediately. Brady Wayne took his time. He put the Colt in its holster, unbuckled his shell belt, and rolled it carefully around the gun before placing it on a grassy spot where the least amount of dust could reach it.

"Molly won't like this half as much as I will," Ed said. His voice was hardly more than a whisper. Warm blood pumped through his veins, bringing back the strength his wounds had sapped away during the past few days. He wanted this fight. He wanted to feel his fists punish Brady Wayne's golden face. He was not sure whether he was fighting for Molly Hill or to avenge his father, but the reason did not matter. He needed to strike back at something, at somebody, and the Skillet foreman had offered himself as a target.

It was going to be a bloody, ruthless fight. Brady Wayne had lived with his own devils, and they had driven him to challenge Ed. He had hinted of hidden grudges and frustrations. He was a failure in his father's eyes, and had a craving for success, even if it had to come through marriage to a wealthy man's daughter. Ed Jessup stood in his way, just as he stood in Morgan Hill's way. Brady Wayne wanted to kill Ed, but the risk was too great, so he would try to beat him into submission.

The Skillet foreman came directly at him, a tawny, hard-muscled man with animal swiftness and a sickly light burning in his eyes. A silent appeal ran through Ed's mind: "Lord, let me last just long enough . . ."

Chapter Nine

Fists cocked, lips thinned, Brady Wayne circled and feinted until he saw an opening, then darted in close and swung a sledging blow at Ed Jessup's cheek.

Ed had been watching for that first charge. He rolled his head aside, back-stepped, and grabbed for the out-stretched arm. He got both hands on Wayne's wrist, but the foreman's other fist slammed against his ear. Ed staggered drunkenly. He shook his head as bells clanged in his ears, but he held on to the arm. He gave a sharp tug, drawing Wayne's head and shoulders toward the ground. At the same time he lifted one knee upward, smashing it against Brady Wayne's nose. The impact made a squishy, gritty sound as bone ground against bone.

The Skillet foreman fell backward, both hands clawing at his smashed nose. Blood spurted between his fingers, staining his shirtfront. Ed grabbed for the fallen man with the ferocity of a cougar, but Wayne scooted away on all fours. He straightened a few feet away, and ran for his horse.

Ed started after him, then stopped, held back by a vagrant thought that warned him to leave well enough alone. Brady Wayne was running, backing away from a fight he had started. That was victory enough for the moment. Ed knew they would meet again. Brady Wayne was no longer just a hired hand who carried out Morgan Hill's orders. He had his own reasons for wanting to run Ed out of the country.

The Skillet foreman reached his horse. He fumbled with the cinch ring and brushed a hand at his bleeding nose. He threw a blood-smeared glance toward Ed and spoke through swollen lips.

"Mind tossing me my gun? I — I've had enough."

Ed retrieved his own gun first. With the Colt balanced in his hand, he turned to look for Wayne's shell belt. Even as he turned, Ed knew something was wrong. He heard the sound, but it took him a split second to recognize the hissing of a thrown rope, and by then it was too late.

With his body shielding his movements, Brady Wayne had taken his rope from the saddle horn and loosened it, and now the loop was settling around Ed Jessup's shoulders, sliding down to pin his arms to his sides. He dropped the gun to try to grab the rope, but he had reacted too slowly. A hard yank from Wayne's hands tightened the loop and threw Ed off balance.

He crashed awkwardly to the ground. It was like bulldogging a steer. Wayne rushed to Ed's side and threw another half hitch around Ed's legs, rendering him helpless.

"You're a damn' fool, Jessup," Wayne grunted. "Nobody ever whipped me that easy. Now you get yours!"

Ed saw the boot coming at him, but had no way to stop it. The swift kick caught him in the ribs. It drove the wind out of him with such force it sickened him. Wayne swore under his breath and came down on top of Ed, knees grinding into his chest. Desperately Ed arched his back, trying to throw the man aside. The effort increased the pain in his lungs and ribs. He fell back, fighting the dizziness.

Brady Wayne shifted his weight and straddled Ed's chest. He smashed a fist against Ed's chin, ripping skin from his cheekbone and bruising his left eye.

Ed had to surrender to the beating. It would not cease until Brady Wayne believed him to be dead or unconscious. He had only to suffer through a few more blows, he told himself, and it would be over, but pride and fury kept him struggling. He thrashed from side to side and tried to free his arms, but Brady Wayne was good with a rope.

He was good with his fists, too, when there was no defense against them. Wayne took his time and aimed his punches with deliberate viciousness. Ed finally stopped struggling. He lay on the ground with the sun burning against his bruised and bloody face, his head rocking from side to side as Wayne beat him. A foggy red haze clouded his vision. His stomach quivered with nausea, but he never quite lost consciousness.

The jolting fists finally stopped landing. Ed heard the scuff of Brady Wayne's boots as the man stood up. He let his muscles go limp as Wayne rolled him over roughly and removed the rope.

There was a slap and hiss of leather as Wayne found his gunbelt and buckled it on. Stirrup leather creaked.

Churning hooves stirred up dust as the Skillet foreman pulled his horse around. He said, "If you stay around here I'm going to waylay you every time I can. I'm going to truss you up like a calf for slaughter and beat the hell out of you every time, and someday, when it looks safe enough, I'll kill you, so if you want to stay alive, Jessup, pick up your money at the bank and get out of Singletree country."

Against the numbness of Ed's mind, Brady Wayne's parting threat was a dull murmur, and he did not feel like replying. It was ten minutes later, after the hoofbeats of the man's horse had faded in the distance, that Ed pushed up on his elbows and stared in the direction of Skillet. Wayne's fists had weakened Ed's body, but they had not weakened his determination. He still meant to face Morgan Hill on his own ground.

Alone and unashamed, Ed groaned aloud. He was not certain whether the outcry was a result of the pain in his body or the anguish born of his own failures. He had vowed to keep his ranch, and Ellen Ditmar believed he was strong enough to lead the other ranchers from Maverick Creek in a fight to reclaim the land they had fled, but so far he had been more of a victim than a leader. His home had been burned, his father killed, and Brady Wayne had beaten him senseless. Despite his misery, however, he found himself strangely concerned that the affection he had seen in Ellen's eyes might turn to disappointment by the time he saw her again.

He did not take Brady Wayne's remarks lightly. They still echoed in his mind and he knew he would have to look over his shoulder from now on. His troubles had started because of Morgan Hill's fear and greed, and they would have to be settled with Hill, but he had another enemy, Brady Wayne, and he considered the Skillet foreman the more dangerous of the two. If he could force Morgan Hill to back down, however, he might find peace again. He doubted that Brady Wayne would have much appetite for a fight without Skillet's backing.

All he could think about right now was to reach Skillet and try to reason with Morgan Hill. He was too battered and angry to think beyond that first step. Rising unsteadily to his feet, he staggered down to the creek and dropped to the ground at the water's edge. He dipped up water with his hands and sloshed it over his head and face, wincing from the sting of the raw places on his skin. Afterward, he crawled into the shade of the cottonwoods. He lay back on the ground, his chest heaving, and wondered if he had enough strength left do anything.

Matt Latham found him that way shortly before noon. Ed's arms were spread on either side of him, and his face was crusted with dried blood. At first, Latham thought he was dead; then he saw the slow rise and fall of Ed's chest. He went to work on the bruised face with a wet handkerchief, and presently Ed opened his eyes. For another few seconds Ed lay without moving, uncertain of his whereabouts; then he slowly sat up, peering at the broad face in front of him, the bristly gray mustache, and deep-set blue eyes.

"It's me, Ed, in case you ain't sure," Latham said. "I was your neighbor up the creek a-ways."

"Yeah, I know." Ed shook his head, trying to clear his mind. "I had a run-in with Brady Wayne a little while ago, and I didn't feel too good when it was over." He gave Latham a brief account of the fight, then grinned weakly. "Glad you happened along, Matt. I needed to see you. I heard you folks were still around town."

Latham's rounded jaws hardened. "We took such work as we could land. Me, I'm clerking some at Lance Barker's General Store. Sam Ditmar is tending bar at Clayton's. Harve Grayson got on as a part-time hostler at McPherson's Livery, and Clay Siler is trying to trap mustangs. We all had a hired hand or two, and most of them are still around, too. Just loafing around town hoping to land a riding job with some outfit."

Latham spread his hands and stared at thick, rope-scarred fingers. "Hell of a way for a cowman to try to earn a living, Ed. Nothing for a man to put his teeth into. More like charity, but we stayed close in hopes we'd get a saddle under us again somehow. We all figured Jericho John could clear up this difficulty with Skillet. Now I don't know what we ought to do. Ellen Ditmar come into town yesterday. She said she ran across you on Mescalero Ridge. She said Jericho John is dead. I'm real

98

sorry about that, Ed — sorry for you and sorry for us."

It was a lengthy speech for a man of Latham's quiet nature, and it ended with a listless shrug. Ed rubbed a palm gingerly across his bruised cheek, looking away as he spoke. "Maybe I made a mistake by talking pa into letting me try to throw off the hobbles Morgan Hill has put on us all these years, but I can't live under another man's thumb. Pa died fighting for his land, and I aim to go on fighting for it. Hill figures he's got us whipped, but if he sees he's got a long battle on his hands, he might leave us alone."

Latham's deep-set blue eyes stared moodily at the ground, and his big hands wrung the last drop of water from the neck scarf. He folded it carefully, then slipped it into the pocket of his frayed town coat. He rose, shaking his head. "I rode out this way because I had a hankering for a last look at my land, but now I don't know why I bothered. It just makes things harder. All of us were counting on your pa to give us some backing, but now that he's dead, it changes things. I figure I might as well drift out of these parts. You can't homestead in Texas, but maybe I can find some homestead land in Arizona Territory. We don't stand much chance without somebody like Jericho John to talk up for us."

Ed studied the thick-bodied cowman, finding him somewhat grotesque in his flat-heeled shoes and peg-legged pants. He said, "Talk never did get us anywhere, Matt. We've been living like Hill is in charge of our own lives — like we're just using the land by his good graces. That's a setup a man like Hill can cancel any time he gets tired of it. As long as you look up to him like he's a king, then he's going to look down on you. He admires men who have made their mark on the West, men with a lot of grit and a fast gun. Maybe that will work to our good. Once he sees we've got some guts and are ready to use our guns he might be inclined to respect our rights."

Latham tilted his head thoughtfully. "What are you driving at, Ed?"

"Just what I said—let Hill know we're going to make our mark on this land, too. Let him know we're too tough for him. I aim to start by rebuilding my cabin and showing Hill I'm not going to run. This ranch is all I've got. I could ramble around the rest of my life and not have this good a start again, so I aim to hold on to it. The way I figure it, once you start giving up things, you can get in the habit of giving up. That's what makes a man a failure. It's a habit I don't want to grow on me."

"And you want the rest of us to hang on with you?"

Ed nodded solemnly, aware of the resistance building in the man's face. Latham was a cautious, hard willed man, and one not easily persuaded to face uncertain risks.

His glance met Ed's eyes. "You've got guts, all right, Ed, but you ain't no Jericho John Jessup. That's plain to see from what happened between you and Brady Wayne, and Wayne is going to keep dogging you, too—both him and Morgan Hill."

Ed shrugged. "Wayne talks tougher than he is. I can beat him in a fair fight, fists or guns. He's trying to make this thing a grudge fight between him and me. Hill's trying to do the same, claiming I'm forcing my attention on Molly and that I shot him on purpose, but he'll have to change his sights if we all stick together. He's bound to have some kind of conscience, and some respect for the law. He's not likely to want the blame for killing everybody on Maverick Creek if that's the only choice we give him."

Doubt was still in Latham's face. He rubbed a forefinger across his mustache. His head swung around and he gazed northward, toward the place he had made his home. There was sadness and yearning in the deep-set eyes, but there was a fear of Skillet's power there, too.

He said, "I don't know what kind of conscience Hill has, maybe a little, maybe none. Some of us was talking in town yesterday about asking him to pay us for our cattle, and even a little for the damage the fires did. That would give us a stake, something to start over someplace else. We were using open range, so we can't sell him land. We were hoping to get enough ahead some day to get deeds for the land, but now I guess—"

"Hill's using more open range than all of us put together," Ed cut in. "That's common practice hereabouts. Until the state land office says different, ranchers figure they're entitled to graze on open range as far out as a cow can walk in one day, but even that's not enough for Hill. Skillet has grown bigger than he ever thought it would and he's running out of graze. That's one reason he wants us out. He offered pa money, but I've got nothing for sale. If he thinks you're going to run, the price comes cheap. He'll give you something for your cows, Matt, but he'll be buying your backbone, too."

Color flooded Latham's lined face and he gave Ed an offended stare. He tugged angrily at his hat brim, rose abruptly, and walked toward his horse.

Ed was aware of the rebuff, but he also could see the rancher's discomfort in the townsman's clothes he had adopted for his job as a clerk in the general store. He remembered the longing in Latham's eyes when the man had looked in the direction of his burned-out ranch.

"Do me one favor," Ed called after him. "Take a vote on it. Let's call the others together and let them decide what we ought to do—fight or run."

Latham's horse stood only ten feet away. Farther on, Ed saw his own buckskin, its reins trailing, where the rancher had left it after leading it closer to the creek. Latham had unsaddled it and loosened the bit so it could graze.

As he climbed into the saddle, Latham turned and

frowned toward Ed Jessup. "You'll find a lot of tempers on edge right now. It might not be hard to start a war if somebody wants to stir one up. That scares me. No matter what you think of me, I'm not a coward. I'd take up a gun in a minute if I didn't believe that it's the worst thing any of us could do. We could all end up dead without proving anything. I'm not a gunfighter and neither are our neighbors. I don't want to be sorry later for causing a lot of people to die."

"Maybe I can settle things with Hill before it goes that far, Matt. I'm going to try, but we've got to show him we're men and not sheepdogs that will start running any time he whistles."

"I'll get word to the others," Latham said, sighing. "They're entitled to hear you out. Where do you want to meet and when?"

"The back room at Clayton's Saloon" Ed stood up slowly, still shaky on his feet. The swelling in his lips had grown and he had to speak slowly to be understood. "I should be there some time around noon tomorrow."

Latham shifted the reins in his fingers and looked at Ed Jessup skeptically. "You ought to ride in with me now and see if Doc Stratton can give you something that'll get your strength back. You may not live till tomorrow. Can't this meeting wait until you're feeling better?"

Ed shook his head. He was bruised and battered, but he had no intention of changing his plans. The agate hardness of the pale blue eyes made its impression on Matt Latham. He did not argue further, nodding silently as Ed said, "I don't want Morgan Hill to rest any easier than we do. I want him to look me in the face and start worrying about us. I want him to back off or get a good notion that he's in for a lot of trouble. I'll talk to a doctor after I meet with you folks in Singletree tomorrow."

After Latham had gone, Ed went deeper into the

102

shade of the cottonwoods, his boots making no sound on the cushion of leaves which had accumulated over the years. He sat with his back against a tree trunk and waited. He had hoped to arrive at Skillet headquarters before full daylight, but he had spent too much time studying the rubble of his cabin. The fight with Brady Wayne had delayed him even more. Most of the Skillet riders would be at the roundup camp near Comanche Draw, but Hill always kept a few hands around to do routine chores at the ranch, and since the day the rancher had decided he was not a suitable suitor for Molly, every Skillet rider had been given orders to keep Ed Jessup away.

Most of the pain caused by Brady Wayne's fists finally wore off, but during the afternoon Ed bathed his face in the cool waters of Maverick Creek to reduce the swelling. It was the gash on his back, suffered during the dragging incident, which caused him the most trouble. As the land around him soaked up the force of the searing sun, the shade of the cottonwoods was not enough to shelter him from the heat of the day, and Ed should have been covered with sweat. Instead he felt cold and shaky.

While he rested, Ed's thoughts turned back to the last time he had visited the Skillet Ranch. It was more than a year ago — the day Morgan Hill found him and Molly in a warm embrace. They had just returned from a Sunday afternoon ride, and were standing next to one of the corrals when he took Molly in his arms to kiss her good-bye.

Unexpectedly Morgan Hill stepped around the corner of a nearby barn and saw them holding each other. The rancher's voice exploded in a string of threatening oaths as he came toward them. Ed pushed Molly away and stood frozen, not knowing what to do or say. He braced himself for a stern lecture from Molly's father, but words were not enough for Morgan Hill at a time like this. He swung a knotted fist at Ed's chin, his breath rasping in his throat. Ed ducked and darted away a few steps, trying to mumble an apology.

The rancher wasn't listening. His booming bass voice filled the air with curses again, the words tumbling one upon the other in such a torrent that a thread of spittle ran down his chin. Ed thought Morgan Hill was going to swing at him again, but Hill grabbed Molly's arm instead and backed her away as though she needed his protection.

When he saw the passion in Molly's eyes, Hill must have realized for the first time that she had grown past girlhood long ago, a beautiful and desirable young woman. For years Hill himself had encouraged their friendship, beginning when they were only youngsters; Ed had served as Molly's escort for the occasional social functions sponsored by their school, and Hill had continued to welcome Ed at the Skillet Ranch. After all, it was good for Morgan Hill's daughter to be seen in the company of Jericho John Jessup's son; but when he saw them with their bodies pressed together and their lips exploring each other, he knew there was more to their relationship than he had ever suspected.

With Molly standing behind him the rancher jabbed a forefinger at Ed and said, "I trusted you, boy, but I can see that you're up to no good! I won't have you taking liberties with Molly! I won't have her being tied up with a ragtag cowboy who'll give her nothing but kids and hard times! Get off my land, Jessup, and don't come back! If you ever step foot on the Skillet again, I'll horsewhip you or — or kill you!"

Two weeks later, Hill shipped Molly off to a finishing school in St. Louis, and Ed had no reason to go near the Skillet Ranch even if he could have mustered the nerve — but he had a reason now, a reason so pressing he had a difficult time waiting for the right moment. Since he had missed arriving at dawn, he needed the cover of dusk to shield his approach.

It was almost a three-hour ride from Maverick Creek to Morgan Hill's headquarters, and in late afternoon Ed mounted the buckskin and rode toward Skillet.

Chapter Ten

The appearance of wealth reflected by the Skillet Ranch could dampen the spirit of any man who lived on the edge of poverty, but the sight of it only honed Ed Jessup's ambition. He wanted a place just as prosperous, and he had a right to try to build something good and lasting from the promise of this yet-untamed Texas range. He would not let Morgan Hill stop him from pursuing that goal!

Morgan Hill's headquarters resembled a small settlement sprawled along the middle of the narrow valley—a scene dominated by a rambling ranch house built of stones which must have taken scores of buckboards to haul from the limestone bluffs three miles away. There was a long, flat-roofed bunkhouse with glass windows and whitewashed log walls, and a scattering of pole corrals with three large barns towering in the background. Between the corrals and the barns was a line of smaller structures: a blacksmith shop, a toolhouse, a carriage shed, and slatted storage rooms.

Ed came within sight of Skillet amid the purple haze which shrouded the prairie for a brief interval between dusk and full darkness. When he was about a hundred yards away from the nearest building, he left his horse behind a screen of brush and continued on foot. Bent low and moving swiftly, he ran from shadow to shadow — from tree to tree, bush to bush, until he finally came up behind the line of storage buildings.

There was no sign of life until he came close to the bunkhouse; then he heard the hum of voices, but it sounded like there were only two or three men inside. His familiarity with the layout of the ranch gave him confidence in the route he chose, but still he felt the vibration of his heart as it beat against his chest.

Most of the Skillet crew would be at the Comanche Draw roundup camp, but Ed knew those left at the ranch would be especially alert because of the events of the past few days. Ed was sure Brady Wayne would be somewhere on the premises. The foreman would have to ride out hours before daybreak to reach the roundup site in time to supervise the day's work, but Brady Wayne would not let that inconvenience interfere with his desire to stay close to Molly Hill every moment he could.

A long gallery porch ran along the west side of the ranch house, shaded by a head-high greasewood hedge which had been transplanted there to blunt the heat of the afternoon sun. After taking a circular path around the bunkhouse, Ed ran across the yard and gained the narrow walkway which separated the greasewood from the gallery. He was breathing hard, more from tension than from exertion. Sweat dripped from the ends of his shaggy black hair, streaking his bronzed face with glistening rivulets.

Slumping to keep his head in the shadows, Ed paused midway along the porch and listened for any sound of activity. Just before he reached the porch, he had seen the orange glow of a lamp in the kitchen area, but that had been in the east wing of the house, now hidden from view. A patch of light was visible

107

twenty feet ahead of him. It came from the end windows of the spacious parlor which traversed the front of the house and connected the two wings of the house to form a square U. Ed guessed that Morgan was probably responsible for the light in the parlor.

Just as he was about to move on, a small flicker of flame directly opposite his position caught his attention. He edged closer to the greasewood, not sure whether he should hurry ahead or remain still. Before he could decide, the flicker blossomed into a spreading light, and Ed saw that he was standing across from an open window. The curtains were drawn back, and he had a clear view of the interior.

He was looking into Molly Hill's bedroom, and when he first saw her she was replacing the glass chimney on a freshly lit lamp set on a table near a high poster bed. Beyond her, in an alcove to her right, a polished brass bathtub shimmered in the lamplight.

As she moved away from the lamp, her body was partially cloaked in the shadows cast by the furniture, but the soft light enhanced the contours of her full breasts and bare shoulders, giving her skin the sheen of pale pink velvet. Apparently Molly had just finished her bath in the dusky darkness, but now needed light to locate her clothes.

She was in no hurry to dress, feeling secure behind the thick foliage which screened her room from the ranch yard. Ed let his breath out slowly. His skin felt hot and the blood rushed to his face. He dropped his glance to the ground, feeling like a thief because of his inadvertent view of Molly's nude body.

His glance still averted, Ed took a step forward, then stopped as someone entered Molly's room. A doorway leading to the hall swung quietly inward, and Ed saw Brady Wayne move across the floor on the balls of his feet, making no sound. Molly had seated herself in front of a mirrored dresser and was running a comb through her blond hair, tilting her head to view the results.

The Skillet foreman had left off his gun and spurs, and there was nothing on his person to rattle and announce his presence. He was bareheaded, his golden hair slightly tousled across his forehead. Even in the dim light, Ed could see the redness of the man's nose and a swollen mound across the bridge of it — the result of the blow Ed's knee had struck earlier that morning. He could also see the sly grin on the man's face as he approached Molly.

He came at her from the side so that his reflection was not visible in the mirror. When he was within four feet of her, one quick step brought him up behind her and his arms went around her bare waist. He bent close, clamping his chin against her shoulder. His hands moved hungrily over her body, caressing her stomach and sliding upward to squeeze her breasts.

Molly's mouth flew open in surprise and Ed thought she was going to scream, but she did not utter a sound. Her bent arm jabbed suddenly backward. The point of her elbow caught Brady Wayne in the pit of his stomach, and Ed heard him gasp for air as the breath went out of him.

Molly took a step to the side and stood erect. Her face was contorted with anger. She swung the heavy hair brush at Wayne's face, but the foreman had recovered almost instantly from the sting of the jabbing elbow. He ducked easily away and reached for Molly again. His voice was clearly audible through the open window.

"Come on, Molly, go to bed with me." A teasing grin played across Wayne's mouth. "You know we're going to be together someday. We're going to be married. Why hold out on me? Why not now?"

Molly's reply came through gritted teeth. "My father will kill you, Brady, if I tell him what you did."

She started toward the poster bed where she had left a blue flannel wrapper lying across the covers. Brady Wayne danced sideways, blocking her path. She tried to go around him, but the foreman cut her off again. A look of desperation clouded Molly's face.

"I've always liked you, Brady, and sometimes I want you, but this isn't one of those times. I don't like sneaky people. Maybe some day I'll marry you, or maybe we'll make love, but I won't do it this way. I won't be forced! Do you hear me, Brady?"

Her voice rose to a high pitch, ringing against the walls. She glanced around, her arms waving as if she were fighting off wasps. She darted back to the dresser, grabbed a small wooden chest, and flung it at Brady Wayne. It sailed over his head and struck the wall with a loud clatter. Two or three small compartments fell out of the chest as it struck the floor and Ed heard the metallic tinkle of jewelry falling about.

Brady Wayne laughed. He extended his arms, beckoning with his hands, and walked purposefully toward Molly again. She backed into a corner, looking around for something else to throw at him.

Until now, Ed had stood frozen in his tracks. He did not want to reveal his presence, and he especially did not want Molly to believe he had been spying on her while she was undressed, but as the Skillet foreman closed in on her, Ed clamped a hand on his gun butt. His pulse was pounding. A few steps and one quick leap would take him through the open window and inside the bedroom. He would be risking his life, but he could not stand by and watch Molly being manhandled.

His heart racing, Ed got ready to spring forward, but he did not have to intervene. Another form loomed in the gray outline of the open doorway, and lamplight bounced off the blued steel of a double-barrel shotgun. Morgan Hill stepped inside. His snow white hair shone like sculptured frost above his weathered face. His coarse black eyebrows were drawn in a solid line over his granite eyes. The butt of the shotgun was planted against a brawny shoulder, its sights lined on Brady Wayne.

The foreman lifted his hands in a restraining gesture and backed across the room, his lips twitching in fear. "Hold up now, Morgan. I didn't do anything. I — I was just teasing Molly some. I got carried away. I'm sorry. It won't happen again. I must've lost my head."

Morgan Hill's expression did not change. He remained silent until Molly had slipped around behind him and grabbed the flannel robe from her bed to cover her nakedness; then he said, "I heard a commotion back here, but I didn't expect to find something like this. I thought it might be that hotheaded Jessup kid, but you, Brady . . . you . . ."

The anger in the rancher's voice was tempered by a tone of sadness. He lowered the shotgun a few inches and shook his head. "I took you on as a favor to your pa. Roscoe Wayne is the best friend I've got, even if I don't see him much. We fought the Mexican War together, and we've been close ever since. Roscoe asked me to take you on afer that last shooting scrape you were in. He thought they were going to hang you if you didn't get away from the Pedernales. He thought you might settle down, and I've sort of took to you myself. I thought me and Roscoe could join our families together through you and Molly. But you're just like that damn squatter Al Burke who set up on Maverick Creek years ago — always trying to ruin a man's womenfolk. You're too wild and mean to treat a woman decent and wait for a marriage before you — "

111

"I just lost my head, Morgan," Wayne said again.

Morgan Hill's eyes narrowed. The sadness was gone, and his voice was full of rage. "If I catch you at something like this again, you're going to lose your guts, Brady. I'm going to scatter them all over the countryside with a shotgun if you ever force your way with Molly. Now get out of here and go about your business. Turn in. We're still working a cattle roundup, you know."

His head bowed, Brady Wayne hurried through the doorway and out of sight. Morgan Hill looked toward his daughter. Molly was tugging self-consciously at the belt which held the robe closed around her.

"Are you all right, honey?"

She nodded, and Hill said, "Don't hold this against Brady. I want him to understand my principles, but I'd still like to have him in the family. It would mean a lot to me. He's a lot better man than Ed Jessup. He's at least got a future to offer a woman."

"I know," Molly said quietly.

Hill patted her shoulder, smiled, and left the room.

Outside, Ed breathed a sigh of relief and crept farther along the hedgerow, eager to be away from Molly's bedroom window. He was puzzled by his own emotions in the aftermath of the scene he had just witnessed. Molly had not rebuffed Brady Wayne as a matter of honor and distaste as Ed had first thought. She had denied him his pleasure because his advances had not come at a time and place of her choosing. He should be upset by Molly's behavior, Ed thought absently. He was surprised that he felt no particular remorse.

Forcing himself to remain patient, he waited until Morgan Hill had time to settle himself in the parlor again. An owl wailed somewhere nearby, and the sound gave Ed a start. He was jumpy. He clenched his

112

teeth and fought against the urge to turn away and come back another time.

He took two deep breaths, gathered his strength, and ran toward the front of the house before he changed his mind. He ducked low to dodge the light from the window, rounded the corner, and stepped softly up on the front porch. With one hand he slipped his gun free. With the other he wrenched at the door latch, found it unlocked, and threw his weight against the panel.

Ed's boots clattered against the planked floor of the large parlor. Lamplight stabbed at his eyes, and he blinked to adjust his vision.

Fifteen feet away, his back toward a gaping rock fireplace, Morgan Hill sat hunched behind a massive oak desk. A ledger book was spread out before him, and the stub of a pencil was gripped in his fingers. The way he sat there, listless, chin lowered, broad shoulders slumped, told Ed that Morgan Hill had lived with uneasy thoughts these past few days.

Hill did not rise. His rock-hard eyes narrowed and his face turned the color of saddle leather as anger warmed his blood. A slight movement of his left hand sent light flashing from the diamond ring on his little finger.

"You've got mighty poor manners, Jessup, and even less sense." Hill's voice was a hoarse whisper. "Brady told me what you did to my daughter out in the mesquite trees. He said he whipped you for it. Now what do you want here?"

"Brady Wayne is a liar," Ed said. "All Molly and I did the day he saw us out on the range was talk. He wants me out of the way, and he's using you to do his dirty work. You want me out of the way, and you're using him to do your dirty work. You want his old man's ranch, or part of it, and he wants Skillet. The two of you are going to trip over each other trying to see who gets what first."

"I asked you what you want here."

The picture of his father tumbling from the saddle, one foot lodged grotesquely in the stirrup, flashed through Ed's mind. He said, "I want to kill you, Hill—that's what I want. I want to kill you for what you did to my pa."

The pencil dropped from the blunt fingers. Hill's fists clenched on the desktop and he shoved his chair away. Slowly he came to his feet, a giant of a man in a blue silk shirt, a man filled with defiance. He took a step forward, his fists still clenched at his sides.

Hill said, "Brady told me about Jericho John. I didn't want that. I'm sorry he's dead, but I didn't kill him. There were nine men up there, and nobody knows whose bullet hit your pa. They went against my orders. I told Brady to see that nobody aimed a shot below the top of the windows, but when you and Jericho John started shooting back, somebody forgot my orders. I just wanted you out of the country. I gave you fair warning. I didn't want anybody killed, least of all Jericho John."

"You ordered the raid, Hill. You have to answer for it."

Hill shook his head in firm denial. "I won't be saddled with that. You can't kill me and nine others just to be sure you get the right man. That will get you hung for murder. It was an accident, just like the slug you put in my shoulder. As far as I'm concerned, I had you bought out. All you had to do was pick up your money at the bank and get out."

Hill paused, his granite eyes still fastened on Ed's face. He shook his head slowly. "You've got your pa's blood, all right. You're nervy, Jessup—maybe plumb mean when you have to be—but you're not going to kill an unarmed man in cold blood."

Ed forced himself to think more rationally. Hill was right; he would not shoot an unarmed man. There was also some logic in the rancher's comparison of Jericho John's death to the accidental shot which had wounded Hill that day in town. Ed had come here to reason with Hill, but an impulsive desire to kill him had taken hold of Ed when memories of his father's death and the suffering Jericho John had endured flooded his mind.

A chill ran along Ed's spine as he realized his own capacity for violence was not much less than that possessed by the man he had sworn to defy.

After a few seconds of silence he said, "You're closer to being dead than you'll ever know. I'd kill you if you had a gun in your hand. You've got some funny notions about what's honest and what ain't, like running a man off his land and then giving him money to make it look good. That won't work with me, but I'll make a deal with you—you like to brag about being fair, a man who never breaks his word—I'm going to build my place back and stay on Maverick Creek. Give me your word you'll leave me alone and I'll get out of your house right now. Otherwise, I'm going to hound you the rest of your life."

Morgan Hill hooked his thumbs inside his tooled leather belt and glared. His eyes narrowed, then widened again. There was no compromise in the set of his face. "You've got the only deal you're going to get from me. Pick up the money I left at the bank for Jericho John and get out of the country. That's my deal. Your gun doesn't scare me. I've got five cowhands here and all I have to do is give them a signal. You fire on me and you'll never leave this place alive. You're a hard-nosed stubborn man, Jessup, but you're no match for—"

The rancher's voice trailed off into a murmur and a gleam of triumph flickered in his eyes. At the same moment, Ed heard the scuffing of a boot behind him. He felt the small hairs on the back of his neck bristle with fear. He wanted to turn around, but he was not sure he should turn his back on Morgan Hill. There was a rifle propped against the end of the oak desk, only two steps beyond the rancher's reach.

Then it was too late to turn.

Cold steel pressed against Ed's back. A gun hammer clicked and a voice said, "Drop the iron, cowboy. Nobody on Skillet takes kindly to seeing a gun aimed at the boss. I was on my way to tell you I was heading out to the roundup camp tonight, Morgan, when I saw him about to —"

"Get out of here, Brady," Morgan Hill cut in sharply. "When I want your help I'll holler." The scene he had witnessed in Molly's bedroom was still fresh in his mind and his irritation with the foreman showed in his voice. "I think I'm about to get my point across to Jessup. I'm giving him a chance to sign a quit-claim deed and settle somewhere else."

Ed relaxed a little as the pressure of the gun barrel left his back. Morgan Hill dismissed Brady Wayne with a wave of his hand, turning his attention back to Ed Jessup. "I'm trying to square accounts for Jericho John, if you've got sense enough to see that. I'm trying to keep you alive — two minutes to get out of this house, another day to get out of the country. If ever I hear of you laying a hand on Molly again, or if you ever pull a gun on me again, I — I'll — "

Brady Wayne's swollen nose made his voice flat and scratchy. His angry curse broke across Morgan Hill's words in "Don't be a sucker, Morgan. I told you what I saw him doing to Molly out in the mesquite. He'll keep panting after Molly like a hound dog unless we

116

teach him another lesson. He's a trespasser here, maybe even trying to steal something. We could shoot him for that."

There was a deliberate purpose behind the foreman's words. He had said just enough to revive Hill's anger — to open old sores which would take a long time to heal. The reminder had the effect he wanted.

Morgan Hill's chest swelled and blood seemed ready to burst a vein which throbbed in his temple. His voice was the deep-throated rumble of a growling dog. "I've had nothing but misery from Maverick Creek. I should have bought up that land years ago. Roust out the cowhands, Brady. We won't shoot this trespasser, but we'll do enough. Take him out by the corral and lay a buggy whip across his back about twenty-thirty times. If we can't beat him enough to make him run, maybe the time *will* come to kill him."

Chapter Eleven

A piercing whistle from Brady Wayne's pursed lips, a calm shift of the gun to keep it aimed at Ed's chest, and Skillet was in command. Boots thumped, spurs jingled, and four big-hatted ranch hands surged into the parlor. Brady Wayne barked orders at them and they closed around Ed Jessup.

His gun was at his feet where he had dropped it when Wayne slipped up behind him. Ed eyed it thoughtfully, debating his chances. If he grabbed for the gun, he might shoot one man, but the other four would riddle him with bullets before he could fire again. He was sure Brady Wayne would like to see him take the gamble.

Ed let the gun lie. It was useless to struggle. He submitted to the rough hands which grasped his arms, pinning them behind him. He went along calmly as they shoved him toward the door. But that was as far as they got with him. A gunshot exploded in the darkness at the other end of the room where the lamps had not been lighted. A shrill whine split the air as a bullet sailed through the open window a few feet to the right of the group moving toward the front door.

Molly Hill came into the light, a shiny .32 pistol in her hand. She was fully clothed now, looking prim and feminine in a checked gingham skirt and starched white blouse. There was a daring, excited gleam in her emerald eyes.

"You're not going to horsewhip him!" Molly shouted. "I walked through the hallway just in time to hear what you want to do. Turn him loose or I'll shoot somebody — not you, Father, but if you make a move I'll shoot somebody else. I don't think you'd like that. Tell them to leave him alone."

Morgan Hill's broad face sagged. "She ain't much with a horse, but she's a good shot, boys. Let's don't make a bad thing worse. We'll take this up another time. Stand away and let him go."

Brady Wayne and the four cowboys shuffled reluctantly toward the desk and stood flanking Morgan Hill. Molly back-stepped toward the front entrance, keeping the gun in a position to cover them. She motioned to Ed Jessup and said, "Pick up your gun, Ed, and come with me."

Ed retrieved the gun, slipped behind Molly, and went outside. She backed out through the doorway and joined him. Ed leaped from the porch and started across the ranch yard at a trot, heading in the direction of his horse. Molly ran up beside him. She grabbed his arm to slow him.

"Wait," she said breathlessly. "They won't shoot. They'll be afraid they might hit me."

Ed stopped, glancing uneasily toward the lighted window. "I appreciate what you did in there, Molly. I'm not sure I could stand any more pain for a while. I'm about done in."

Molly's bosom rose and fell with her heavy breathing. "I want you to leave Texas, Ed. Take the money my father has offered. I'll go with you. We could go to New Orleans. I hear it's fascinating. All the women wear elegant gowns and the men still fight duels there. We could —"

119

"Stop thinking like a little girl, Molly. Gunfights and duels and people busting up each other with their fists ain't the kind of fun you think it is, not for the people mixed up in it." He put his hands on her shoulders, troubled because he no longer understood her nor felt the desire to draw her close to him. "We can't run and hide just to have a good time. That's good for a few weeks or a few months, but I'm looking at a lifetime, and it's here — not in New Orleans or anywhere else. I'm staying here."

"Please listen, Ed." Her voice trembled. She seemed near tears. "I don't want you dead. That's what I'm thinking about. I don't want my father dead, either, or taking the blame for killing you."

"That's not likely to happen. Your pa's smart enough to keep the blame for any killing off his head, but someday I'll have to kill Brady Wayne. He's going to force it. I think it was his voice I heard telling the Skillet riders to keep shooting low enough to kill us when he had us trapped in the house — but your pa sent him there."

"Oh, Ed." Her arms reached for him, but he dropped his hands and pulled away. "I've got to go, Molly. Thanks for helping me."

He turned his back on her and hurried off in the darkness toward the brush patch where he had ground-tied his horse. He had promised Ellen Ditmar he would come to Singletree tomorrow, and he needed all the rest he could get before he met with Matt Latham and the other ranchers.

That night Ed Jessup slept on his own land again. After the ride back from Skillet, he crossed Maverick Creek near the spot where he had fought Brady Wayne. Anchoring the buckskin on a picket line so it could graze, he spread his bedroll near the whispering waters of the stream.

For a long time he lay on his back, staring at the star-

120

lit sky and reviewing in his mind his clash with Morgan Hill. As it turned out, his ride to Skillet had served no real purpose. He had grown up with a father who had spent half his life wearing a badge, and respect for the law was ingrained in Ed's nature. He was too familiar with the informal creeds of western justice to believe there was enough evidence to pinpoint Morgan Hill as his father's killer.

Although grief and fury had almost driven him to kill Morgan Hill, that had not been the motive for his visit to Skillet. He had hoped his boldness would convince Morgan Hill he was not afraid—that he would never give up and run. He wanted Hill to weigh the consequences of a long, drawn-out battle and to become sufficiently discouraged to let the feud die.

He should have known better. Morgan Hill was a man accustomed to having his own way—a man who believed the strong had a right to prevail over the weak. By some odd quirk, he associated Ed's attention to Molly with the memory of a squatter named Al Burke who had won the love of Hill's young wife years ago.

Unable to sleep, Ed sat up on his blankets and fished tobacco and papers from a pocket to roll a smoke. In the distance, a coyote bayed mournfully. Closer by he heard the lowing of the cattle he and his father had bunched farther back on the flats a week ago.

The cattle needed his attention, and he felt frustrated because he did not have time for them. Soon the steers would start drifting, scattering all over the range, and the grueling work of rounding them up would have to be repeated. It might be a long time before he was working cattle again. He had hoped his quarrel with Morgan Hill could be settled between the two of them, but now it threatened to become a full-scale range war.

Ed shuddered, wondering if his confrontation with Morgan Hill had made things better or worse. He crushed out the cigarette and lay back on the blankets. His thoughts drifted back to happier times, to the day he and his family had moved to the Singletree range — a time when life had looked so bright.

They had come with two saddle horses and a buckboard loaded with everything they owned. Jericho John Jessup sat tall and proud, his eyes shining with anticipation as he handled the reins of the team which pulled the buckboard.

On the other side of the wagon seat was a petite, golden-haired woman whose calm voice had cheered her husband during the long ride. Ed had sat between them, a cowlicked boy of ten whose pale eyes darted curious glances over the land which was to be their home.

John Jessup had come ahead months before to select a homesite and build a cabin. It was not completely finished when he brought Ed and his mother to Maverick Creek, but it was far enough along to be comfortable.

They were just beginning to unload their possessions when they had a visitor. Ed still remembered his first look at Morgan Hill — the massive shoulders, the rumbling voice, the haughty confidence with which he sat the saddle of a sleek black stallion. Riding behind him, her small arms clinging to his waist, was a cotton-haired girl of nine.

Morgan Hill was in good spirits. He swept off his hat, surveyed Laura Jessup's trim figure approvingly, then introduced himself.

"And this pretty little thing with me," he said as he stepped from the saddle and swung the girl to the ground, "is my daughter Molly."

Ed's father extended his hand. "This is my son Edward, my wife Laura, and I'm—"

"Hell's fire, man," Hill interrupted, "if I didn't recognize Jericho John Jessup I'd be ashamed of myself! I know all about you and I've looked forward to making your acquaintance. Some may think it's strange, but I've got a drawer full of newspaper clippings and my own notes about gents like you. I heard from one of the men who was doing work on your cabin that you were coming. I wanted to be here to tell you I'm pleased to have you as a neighbor."

He shook John Jessup's hand again. "My, my! Jericho John Jessup in the flesh!"

The two men chatted for a while. Molly Hill hung back, peeping around her father's legs at Ed Jessup. Hill offered to help unload the wagon, giving John Jessup a hand with such heavy items as the iron cookstove and a bulky clothes chest.

When the work was done, Laura Jessup apologized for not being able to invite the rancher for supper or to offer him some dessert and coffee.

"I'll bring one of my fruit pies over to your wife as soon as we're settled," she said. "It's the least I can do in return for your kindness."

Morgan Hill's face clouded. "I've got no wife. Molly's mother has been gone for nearly five years."

The rancher's amiable manner abruptly changed. He stopped and appeared uninterested in further conversation. Shortly thereafter, he said his good-byes, gathered Molly in the crook of his arm, and rode away.

It was nearly two months later, after they had become well enough known to share in rangeland gossip, that the Jessups learned what had happened to Morgan Hill's wife.

From the sadness in his eyes and the abrupt change in his manner that day, they had assumed Hill's wife had died, and that he was still grieving for her, but the truth was more surprising.

John Jessup first heard the story from a liveryman in Singletree, and he shared it with his family. Morgan Hill had started Skillet from a land grant of twenty thousand acres, awarded him for service to the Texas Republic. He claimed preemption rights to another eighty thousand acres of open range because he was the first to graze cattle on it. By the time Jane Malone arrived in Singletree five years later to open a school, Morgan Hill had triumphed over renegade Indian raids, summer droughts, and winter blizzards, and was regarded as a man destined for power and wealth.

The pretty schoolteacher was attracted to the proud cattleman from the moment she met him, and Morgan Hill fell in love with her. A year later they were married. After Molly was born, Morgan and Jane Hill were viewed as the ideal ranch couple, but a woman married to Morgan Hill led a lonely life. Jane Hill often mentioned to others how much she missed the busy social life she had enjoyed before she left her home in the bustling Tennessee river town of Memphis.

Morgan Hill was too busy to worry about a woman's boredom. He was so intent on carving out an empire from the Texas plains that he gave every detail of the Skillet operations his personal attention, even accompanying his crew on the long trail drives to market his cattle.

When he was not engaged in ranch work, he used his spare time to pursue his interest in the violent lives of those who earned their living with a gun. He would spend weeks on horseback or days riding a stagecoach to visit the scene of a gunfight or an armed robbery — especially if it involved such well-known names as King Fisher, Clay Allison, Wyatt Earp, or Jericho John Jessup.

He knew Jane grew lonely in the isolated ranch house, and folks in town recalled that he had appeared pleased when the first settlers opened the graze beyond Skillet's boundary on Maverick Creek. They would move on before long, he predicted, but in the meantime, the womenfolk would provide company for his wife. It was too late to mend his own habits when he learned his wife's frequent visits across Maverick Creek were not for conversation with the settlers' wives, but to enjoy the companionship of a lover.

Hill never suspected that his wife was unfaithful until the day she left him. He learned of her secret in a note she left behind. It had been pinned to Molly's nightgown, and was found by the Mexican housekeeper when she woke the little girl for supper. The Mexican woman gave it to Morgan Hill late that night when he finally came in from the range, and later revealed its contents to about everyone she knew. Jane Hill's letter told Hill that she had been seeing a man named Al Burke for several months, and that she was in love with him. She was leaving with Al Burke for California.

No one knew if Hill reached the squatter's place before Jane and Burke made their getaway, or if they escaped unharmed. A freighter had been unloading the household goods of a new family when Hill arrived at the creek, and his account of that night had been passed along by word of mouth through the intervening years.

The freighter told of a band of Skillet riders sweeping through the night like crazed demons with a yelling, screaming, cursing Morgan Hill in the forefront. Fiery torches sailed through the darkness. Guns roared and children screamed and scattered. Innocent men pleaded for mercy while the flames swept up and down the creek for miles. By morning all the settlers had pulled out, and no one in Singletree had ever seen Jane Hill again.

Afterward, Hill had passed the word that he would kill any man who tried to settle on the land north of Maverick Creek, and no one had dared challenge him until Jericho John Jessup moved in and started the Triple J Ranch. Armed with legal deeds and a reputation which Morgan Hill admired, John Jessup had established his ranch without a fight, and his success gave others the nerve to follow him.

It was a different time and a different situation now, Ed told himself ruefully as he tossed in his blankets. He had no fame or reputation which would hold Morgan Hill at bay. He would have to do it with his gun.

The sounds of stamping horses and creaking wagon traffic aroused Ed from a half-stupor. Singletree was spread out below him, a cluster of sun-dried buildings huddled at the foot of a sloping plain and divided by four crisscrossing wagon roads which served as streets.

He swallowed hard to moisten his throat, blinked his eyes, and forced his mind to become alert. From midnight until sunrise he had slept soundly, but he awoke with fever burning his face and his teeth chattering with chills. After breakfast he spent a long time bathing in the creek, hoping to reduce his temperature, but it had not helped much.

Once on the trail, heading south and west toward town, he had permitted the buckskin to follow its own head. He waited until the horse was well along Main Street before he took control of the reins. He patted the horse's neck and kneed it around to come up in front of Clayton's Saloon.

His slack fingers dropped the reins to the ground near the tie-rail and his feverish eyes fixed on the batwing doors. Wearily, Ed lifted a leg across the saddle to dismount. He stumbled, going to one knee beside the buckskin, and groaned softly.

A man in shiny moleskin pants and a hide vest stepped off the boardwalk, staring with more than casual interest at the fallen rider with the black hair and the ugly bruises on his face. He retrieved Ed's hat from the dirt and set it back on his head.

Ed got up on one knee, but seemed unable to move any farther. The man in the hide vest reached down to help him to his feet.

Something in the rider's pale eyes caused the man to straighten and reconsider. Ed's faintness had worn off quickly. He grabbed hold of his saddle's dangling stirrup and pulled himself upright.

He said to the man, "Much obliged, friend," and took a step toward Clayton's front door.

"Hold up, Jessup. I want a word with you."

Ed looked closely at the man for the first time, and saw the metal star pinned to his shirt pocket beneath the hide vest. He had never met Sheriff Ray Felton, but he had heard enough about him to recognize him.

"I can see you're a mite under the weather," Sheriff Felton drawled, "but this won't take but a few minutes. We need to get some things straight between us. Come along with me over to the town marshal's office."

Before Ed could reply, Sam Ditmar came through the batwing doors of the saloon and stood in front of the sheriff. He had a barman's white apron tied around his waist.

"Can't you see this man needs a doctor, Sheriff?" Ditmar took hold of Ed's arm. "Hold on to me and I'll get you over to Doc Stratton's place."

Ed pushed Ditmar's hand away. "I'll be all right, Sam. This is the man I want to see. If you want to be helpful, get the ranchers together for me. Tell them to wait in the back room at Clayton's. I'll be back here directly."

As Ed turned to follow the sheriff along the boardwalk, Ditmar gave him a searching stare. "I'll get them, but I don't know what good it will do."

The town marshal's office was only three doors up

the street, but Ed's legs were wobbly and he moved slowly as he followed the sheriff. When they were inside, Sheriff Ray Felton eased into a chair and propped his feet up on Marshal Dan Plover's spur-ravished desk. Ed sat on a wood stool across from him and ran his glance around the cluttered room.

"If you're looking for Marshal Plover, he ain't up and about yet," the sheriff said. "He was up for a while this morning, but he asked me to keep an eye on things while he takes a nap in the back room. The way he looks, I figure he was hitting the bottle pretty hard last night."

"Plover's the town joke," Ed said. "I don't care about him. You're the man I've been wanting to see. I want to know what you're going to do about Morgan Hill having my pa killed and burning us out."

Felton grunted and let his feet drop to the floor. He was a tall, stringy man with a solemn, angular face and a reputation for tailoring his brand of law to fit rangeland custom rather than the legal statutes. He had a habit of chewing his fingernails, and he bit at the tip of his forefinger while he measured the anger in Ed's face.

"Well, now," the sheriff said, "don't sound so almighty put upon, son. The way I hear it you ain't exactly been spending all your time in church. There are two sides to every cow chip."

"I don't have time to talk about cow chips, Sheriff. I asked you a straight question and I want a straight answer."

"Just hold your horses," Felton said irritably. "I just want to hang this dirty wash out in the daylight so we both can take a look at it and you'll see what I'm up against." He bit at another fingernail and spat a fragment to the floor. "Morgan Hill is just as upset about this fracas as you are. He sent a rider over to Mesa Springs last night to fetch me. I got to Morgan's place

128

about sunrise and spent an hour talking to him before I rode on into Singletree. I was going to spend the day trying to run you down, so it's handy you showed up here."

"I should have figured on this," Ed said flatly. "Morgan Hill always gets the first lick. He wants to be sure you see things his way."

Felton shrugged. "You tell me what part of this is a lie. Hill says he's told you to quit chasing after his daughter, but you won't pay him no mind. He says you shot him in the shoulder for no reason. Then he tells me you broke into his house and threatened to kill him. Looks like he's put up with a lot from you."

Ed heaved a sigh of disgust. "He didn't tell it all. He dragged me until I was almost dead. Brady Wayne roped me and beat the daylights out of me. Hill burned my home and killed my pa. I want you to arrest him for that."

"Well, now," the sheriff drawled, "Hill filled me in pretty good. I picked you out on the street because I knew how you got the bruises. Hill dragged you because you shot him. Brady Wayne whipped you because you jumped Molly's body out in the bushes. A man has a right to try to get rid of bothersome neighbors when they threaten him and his family. Folks in these parts always agree on that. Hill says he offered to buy you out, but you wouldn't leave. He sent his cowhands out to shoot up your place to let you know you ain't welcome anymore. That's been done before, but things got out of hand and Jericho John got killed in the ruckus. Nobody knows who fired the shot that killed him. You can see where that leaves me."

Ed's throat swelled with fury. His surging emotions renewed his strength and he pushed to his feet. "Look at me, Sheriff. Go look at the ashes of my home, of Matt Latham's, Sam Ditmar's, and the others. Go look

129

at my pa's grave and then tell me who's a bad neighbor. Hill didn't tell you about his big plans — how he wants to own spreads all over Texas and as far as Colorado. That's the reason he wants my land. He thinks he can do as he pleases on this range and buy my land whether it's for sale or not. I didn't take his money and I didn't sign a deed. That land is mine and I aim to keep it as long as I'm alive."

His voice cracked and he paused to get control of himself. He fumbled in his pocket and withdrew the crumpled roll of blood-stained bills he had carried with him ever since he and his father fled the burning cabin. He laid the money on the desk next to Felton's elbow. "Somebody killed my pa and somebody has to answer for it. There's almost seven hundred dollars there. That's a reward for the man who killed my pa."

"Put your money away, son." The sheriff's voice sounded tired. "You ought to sign that deed and find you a quiet place to live. It's hard to win against a man like Morgan Hill."

Ed crammed the money back into his pocket. "It's your job to protect my property."

Sheriff Ray Felton shook his head slowly. "I ain't got time to ride boundary for you or for anybody else. This difficulty you've got with Morgan is a sort of family feud. Texas lawmen don't mix in that sort of thing much. Things get worse when we do. We just let it work itself out — but I won't stand for a man being shot in the back, his cattle rustled, or his womenfolk being mistreated. I'll look into that when the feuding's over."

The conversation with the lawman was not going the way Ed wanted. He was frustrated by the futility of it. His shoulders drooped and he shrugged hopelessly. He said, "It's plain you're not going to do anything, Sheriff. I guess what I've heard about you is true. Folks say you're Morgan Hill's man."

He expected the remark to draw an angry rebuttal, but Felton simply looked up and met his glance. "That's partly right. Morgan asked me to run for sheriff, loaned me the money to make my election bond, and got me a lot of votes. I'll do him some favors as a friend, but I won't change my notion of the law to suit him. He's ready to end this thing — to buy you out and let you go. That would keep peace here."

"That would make your job nice and easy," Ed said bitterly. "Are you telling me Hill has rights and I don't?"

The harshness in Ed's voice did not alter the expression on the lawman's face. "A right to settle on your land, yes — a right to start a war, no. If you keep on trying to get even with Skillet and draw the others into it, I'll need an army to stop the bloodshed, and I ain't got an army. When you go riding on Skillet and start killing people, I won't choose sides. That'll be you starting a range war. I'll come for you and I'll see that you hang or spend a long time in jail."

Ed had no desire to argue further with the man, knowing it was useless. He understood the hard choices this lean, graying man had to make while trying to bring a semblance of order to an area which mocked the power of a single badge and a lone gun. His understanding did not make him feel any better about the situation, but his anger had waned and his voice was calm as he said, "I won't go after Skillet just to get even, but what if they ride on the Triple J again? I'm going to build my place back on Maverick Creek. What happens if I kill Morgan Hill defending my land?"

The sheriff tugged at his hat brim and looked out the window while he considered the question; then he walked around the desk and laid his hand on Ed's shoulder. "I've got a sister who's dying over in Mesa Springs and I want to be with her to the end. Don't come running after me when you think you've got more than you can handle. I'll decide when I need to look into this thing again. It's a forty-mile ride back to my sister's house, and I'll be pondering this mess all the way."

"You didn't answer my question," Ed said.

"I'm getting to it. I've warned you not to ride on Skillet and you'd be wise to mind me . . . but, if they try to burn you out again . . . well, that's the way feuds go. A trespasser found dead somewhere has got no law on his side, the way I see it."

"Then that's the way it'll be," Ed said.

Without looking again at the sheriff, he went outside and headed up the street to Clayton's Saloon, where the other ranchers were waiting for him.

Chapter Twelve

One at a time, they drifted into the back room of Clayton's Saloon. They came with the soft step and muted whispers of men attending a funeral service.

Ed Jessup had no strength to waste on words of welcome or idle talk. He sat in a chair at the end of the long felt-covered table which Hal Clayton reserved for quiet dinners with his friends or private poker games. He looked somewhat pale and weak as he nodded greetings to the men who joined him at the table. Occasionally he sipped at the glass of beer which Clayton had pushed into his hand when he paused at the bar to thank the saloon man for the use of the room.

After awhile, Matt Latham came in and ran his deep-set eyes over the crowd. He wiped the sweat from his face with a bandanna and said, "Looks like we're all here," and sat down in a chair next to Ed.

Speaking quietly, Ed said, "Some of you might think I brought all this trouble down on your heads. I hope not. If you'll think about it, you'll see I haven't done anything I shouldn't be allowed to do. I have a right to buy cattle. I have a right to court any full-grown woman who's old enough to choose her own company, and I have a right to shoot at any man who's trying to kill me. Hill queered my deal to buy breed

133

stock. He says I'm not to speak to his daughter, and he's trying to brand me as a killer because a splinter of lead bounced off Brady Wayne's gun and hit him in the shoulder."

Ed took a sip of beer and continued. "These are the excuses Hill's using to start a war against us, but the rest of you didn't do anything to him. The worst part of it is, none of us has ever done anything except try to walk soft around him and not ruffle his feathers. My pa and the rest of you thought that was a smart plan. You thought it was working because Hill left us alone, but kissing Hill's boots didn't work. He left us alone only because he figured he had us under his thumb and could get rid of us any time he wanted. He . . . uh, he—"

Ed's voice faded to a whisper. He was having difficulty organizing his thoughts. Someone far back in the room called out anxiously, "Are you all right, Ed?"

He nodded, cleared his throat, and rubbed a hand across his eyes. He remained silent a minute, then went on. "Hill just bided his time—waited until he had a need for our land. He needs it now, and he thinks he's bossed us around so long we don't dare buck him. If we had acted like men with some guts at the start he might have been afraid to tackle us, but we didn't, and now we've got to stand up to him and fight for what's ours. We've got as much right to a big house and money in our pockets as Hill has, but we'll never have anything if we give up. I'm going back to Maverick Creek and fight Skillet for as long as it takes. I want all of you to go back with me. If you don't, I'll go it alone. I'm not going to let Morgan Hill prove he's a better man than I am. He might kill me, but it won't be while I'm hiding from him."

The speech was longer than Ed had intended and the effort left him feeling drained. He braced his elbow on the table, rested his chin in the cup of his hand, and waited for the ranchers' response. A murmur of discussion ran through the group, but they were exhanging their views among each other in low tones and whispers, and Ed could not hear what was being said.

"You're making tough talk," a man growled, "but right now you look like a loser. Maybe you ought to tell us who beat the hell out of your face, then explain why we should let you lead us in a fight against Skillet."

Ed's red-rimmed eyes sought out the speaker. It was Clay Siler, the burly, black-bearded cowman who had ridden an emigrant wagon into Texas from Ohio and who now was trying to earn food money by trapping wild mustangs. He sat next to Matt Latham, who seemed to be nodding his approval of Siler's comment.

A roaring sound in his head was numbing Ed's mind. He knew he did not have time for lengthy explanations. He said to Siler, "We've got more important things than my face to talk about. It ain't so much what you think of me that counts right now as what you think of yourself. I just want to know how that shapes up."

Siler turned his head away and Ed studied the other faces in the room, trying to read some support in them. No one seemed to want to look at him. Sam Ditmar, sharp featured and scholarly looking, was staring at the opposite wall. Across from him, his round face glistening with sweat, Harve Grayson sat picking at a loose thread around a button on his shirt.

His concentration on the men around the table almost caused Ed to overlook two people who stood near the doorway to the barroom, their shoulders touching. The jingling of a roweled spur drew his glance in that direction, and he was somewhat surprised to see Ellen Ditmar standing there. Apparently she had excused

135

herself from her job at the Drover's Pride dining room. A red-and-white checked apron was still tied around her slender waist, lending a dash of color to the drab gray dress she wore. He nodded in response to her smile. His eyes told her he was happy she had come.

"Something wrong with us being here, mister?"

The question came from the man beside Ellen Ditmar. He was a tall, muscular youngster with a lean-jawed, handsome face and a cocky manner. He looked to be about the same age as the girl beside him, but his defiant brown eyes had seen much more of life. Feeling light-headed, and eager to be finished with the meeting, Ed started to ignore the question, even though he was aware he had invited it by staring at the pair too long.

As he gave the man a closer look, however, irritation started his pulse throbbing faster. Ellen Ditmar's companion was too arrogant and too eager to be noticed to impress Ed favorably. The way he wore his black-handled gun pushed forward on his leg was like a boast. For the first time, Ed noticed there were four or five cowhands ranged along the wall, and they, too, were eyeing the man with curiosity.

"Who're you?" Ed asked bluntly.

His wide, sloping shoulders shrugged pretentiously, and his slender hands moved along the glistening shell belt until his thumbs were hooked in his waistband.

"We met a long time ago when we were kids. I'm Lonnie Grayson, one-time squatter on Maverick Creek. I got back to these parts just after my old man's place was burned to the ground. That didn't surprise me much. I had a feeling something like that would happen someday. What does surprise me is that this much time has passed and nobody has throwed down on Skillet yet."

136

A nod came from Ed Jessup. Lonnie Grayson, he remembered, had been wild and rebellious by the time he was fifteen, and before he was seventeen had drifted away to seek more excitement than the routine drudgery of his father's small spread could offer. Somewhere he had found it.

At first glance Ed had spotted the notch cut into the butt of Lonnie Grayson's gun, a symbol used by some gunmen to boast of a killing. The sight of it filled him with disdain, and he felt an instant dislike for Harve Grayson's brazen son. Why had Lonnie Grayson chosen this time to return to Singletree? Had he finally grown up enough to realize his rightful place was with his father, helping him build a better life for his family, or was it because he sensed the excitement of violence on Maverick Creek and wanted to be part of it?

Ed was too tired to speculate, and he was ready to dismiss Lonnie Grayson from his mind when the man said sharply, "Somebody was asking you a question when you started reading my brand, Jessup. They wanted to know who beat hell out of you? If you're bringing any more trouble on us, we've got a right to know."

From Lonnie Grayson's curling lips the question became an insult and anger stiffened Ed's back. He set his hands against the table and started to rise, but Matt Latham's thick hand restrained him.

"It's a fair question, Ed," Latham said. "I know what happened, but the others have a right to know, too. They need to know what kind of crowd we're up against. Your pa's rep kept us safe on Maverick Creek for a long time, but like I've said before, you ain't no Jericho John."

The buzzing noise again filled Ed's head, almost drowning out Matt Latham's voice. It had bothered him since morning, and he wondered how much longer he could keep his senses.

At last he said, "I got these lumps on my face when Brady Wayne sneaked a lasso around me while my back was turned. He beat me up, but he didn't scare me off—there's a big difference."

"I know about Brady Wayne." Lonnie Grayson's voice was laced with excitement. He took a few steps away from Ellen Ditmar, walking in short, choppy strides like a strutting rooster. "I was riding the grub line down in the Perd'nals country last year. At roundup time I signed on as an extra hand with an outfit called the Snaketrack. It belongs to Roscoe Wayne, Brady's father. The Snaketrack riders told me plenty about Brady Wayne."

"Like what?" Sam Ditmar asked dryly.

"He's a killer," Lonnie Grayson said, looking pleased that his information had made him the center of attention. "Brady killed a freighter in a saloon fight over a girl, and some say the man never did reach for a gun. There was talk of a hanging, but his old man fixed it with the sheriff and he got off. Later on, he killed one of Snaketrack's cowhands during a bunkhouse poker game. The slug hit the cowboy in the back. Brady swore it was because the man turned on him, acting like he was giving up while he was really going for his gun. It didn't look that way to the other hands, and the Snaketrack crew was talking about dragging Brady out some night and stringing him up themselves. Old Roscoe had seen lynchings before, so he got Brady out of the country before anything could happen. I reckon that's when he came to Skillet."

"I don't care what happened at Snaketrack," Clay Siler snorted. "I care about us."

Lonnie Grayson glared at the black-bearded rancher. "So do I. I'm just pointing out that Brady Wayne is bad medicine and that Ed Jessup ain't no

138

match for him. Nobody's told me straight out yet what started this mess — what set Skillet off and caused Hill to run my old man and the rest of you off your land."

"You must not have been listening good," Ed said softly, keeping his eyes on Lonnie Grayson. "I've told all there is to tell, and I'm sure your pa has, too. Hill has built up some grudges against me so he can make it look like he's got a good reason to run me out."

"So it's your fault," Lonnie Grayson sneered. "You've got us into a war because you've got a hankering for Molly Hill."

Ed turned back to the men sitting around the table near him, choosing to ignore Lonnie Grayson. "Hill looks at me as the biggest threat, I guess. He can't be sure about what Molly might do. She would ruin his plans if she married me."

He talked on for a few minutes, recounting what Molly had told him of Morgan Hill's friendship with Roscoe Wayne and of Hill's plans for expanding his empire. He also told them of Molly's role in the scheme, and of Hill's fervent hope that she would marry Brady Wayne as a way of uniting Skillet and the Snaketrack.

"Brady's not sure how his old man will take all this," Ed said. "He wants to marry Molly so he'll end up owning Skillet himself someday if Hill's plans don't work out. He made that plain to me before I fought him."

Ed sighed and shook his head. "All in all, I guess I'm to blame that things happened when they did. If I had stayed away from the stage station that day, Hill wouldn't have been hit by that piece of lead. I think that's what made him decide it was time to get rid of us. I guess it does boil down to being my fault."

Ed's voice carried a note of sadness as he stopped talking. He sat silently, expecting to hear chairs scrape the floor and booted feet stamp angrily out of the room as a result of his admission, but the men kept their seats, and Harve Grayson cursed under his breath.

Clay Siler was the first to speak. He ran a hand through his thick beard and said grimly, "Morgan Hill must have gone loco when he found out what it feels like to be shot. He figures he's above that, but a man who'll take his spite out on innocent folk is full of the devil."

He set his owlish eyes on Ed Jessup and clucked at the look of guilt on the battered face. "Don't blame yourself too hard, Ed. A personal difficulty ought to be kept personal. If Hill had just burned you out, he might call this thing a feud between you and him, but he hit us all, and his talk about grudges won't hold water. You're right about him, Ed. He wants our land. He wants to be big and famous. I hold him responsible for what happened to my place — nobody else."

Encouragement was what Ed needed, and he was grateful for Clay Siler's support, but he needed more than a defense for his conscience.

"Then you'll go back with me, Clay?"

Siler turned his head aside, avoiding Ed's glance. He fiddled with his belt buckle and tightened his lips.

"No," said Siler. "I didn't say that, Ed. I was run off a place on the Brazos before I came here. I want to be sure I can stay next time. I — I just can't go through that again."

A man cleared his throat, and feet shuffled impatiently along the floor. "Maybe," said Harve Grayson, "we ought to take a vote and be done with it. I don't take much to shoveling manure and throwing down horse feed, but that's my living for the time being. If I don't get back to the livery soon, McPherson might not let me even do that no more."

Before anyone else could speak, Lonnie Grayson strode across the floor and stopped beside the table. He flipped his cream-colored Stetson to the back of his head and shook aside a lock of curly brown hair.

"I say we ought to give Hill a dose of his own medicine," he said. "Not sit on our tails like a bunch of old women and wait for Skillet to start running cattle on our land. Jessup's notions don't make sense. He wants to creep out there and build our houses back so Hill can burn them down again, and that's what he'll do if we don't strike first. We can get enough men together to tear his place apart. Pa had two riders helping at our place, and they're back there next to the wall now. Sam Ditmar had a rider and Clay Siler had one. I've been talking to them, and they'll fight with us. We don't want to go back to Maverick Creek like Jessup says, and shake in our boots until Hill comes again. I say we ought to hit Skillet with some guns and torches, and get Morgan Hill to guarantee us peace in writing. Then we'll build again. I want to ride on Skillet now."

"No!" Ellen Ditmar's voice was loud and fearful. Ed looked at her and saw in her eyes a plea for reasoning. "Lonnie has always been a hothead. He'll get you all killed if you listen to him. You'd better listen to Ed."

As faces turned toward her in surprise, Ellen blushed and glanced apologetically at her father, knowing how he felt about women interfering in men-talk. "I—I'm sorry," she murmured, stepping back against the wall.

"Ellen is right," Ed said. "Things are at a standstill now, and nobody is shooting at anybody, but if we go riding on Skillet we're going to be blamed for starting something that can get out of hand. Sheriff Felton told me a few minutes ago he's going to be after me if a range war breaks out, but if Skillet comes after us again, he expects us to defend our property. We need to fight Skillet on our own land if we can, and if there's no fight, we'll be even better off."

"You ain't got guts enough to lead a raid on Skillet!" Lonnie Grayson yelled from the back of the room. "That's the size of it, Jessup! You let them kill your pa and you ain't man enough to do anything about it!"

Ed's face colored. "I don't know which Skillet man killed my pa, but I've got a good notion about who gave the orders to shoot low enough to hit him. That was Brady Wayne, and it was against Hill's orders. I don't have to organize a raid to settle that score. When the time is right, I'll settle it. It's none of your business, Lonnie."

Lonnie Grayson opened his mouth to continue the exchange, but Harve Grayson turned a withering glance toward his son and said, "Shut your smart mouth, Lonnie." To the others he said, "Let's take a vote. If the rest of you want to go back to Maverick Creek, I'll go."

"I doubt we need to vote," Matt Latham said thoughtfully. He tugged at the lapels of his frayed frock coat and turned tentatively as if to speak to Ed, then stared at the floor. "Everybody who wants to go back and buck Skillet stand up."

In the silence that followed, the tinkling of glasses in the barroom beyond the dividing wall was loud and distracting. Outside, a freighter cursed furiously at his team, and somewhere farther along the street a woman was calling for her children to come to dinner.

In the back room at Clayton's saloon not a man moved. Ed Jessup put his hands on the table and shoved himself erect.

"All right," Ed said. "I promised my pa I'd hold on to our ranch if I had to kill one Skillet man at a time to do it. None of you men started this fight, and you don't have to go on with it. I'll go back alone. The rest of you can join me if you change—"

Ed could not finish the sentence. His senses reeled, and the faces around him were blotted out by a swirling gray fog. He had used up the core of his body, and the grief and anger which had kept him going for more than a week could no longer offset the fever and fatigue. Before he began crumpling to the floor, he murmured again, "I'll go alone. . . ."

He woke up in a room at the Drover's Pride Hotel with purple twilight filtering through the dust-coated windows and a coal-oil lamp flickering in the rack above his head. Doctor Wade Stratton, fat and wheezing, and smelling of pungent medications, sat on the edge of the sagging mattress, two fingers of one hand grasping Ed's wrist.

Sensing Ed's gaze on him, Doc Stratton released his wrist and grunted. "So you're finally awake. You've been knocked out for nigh seven hours, but that was good. While you was unconscious I forced a little laudanum down your gullet. I got the cook downstairs to heat up the little iron rod I carry around for things like this, ran it over that gash on your back, and burned away some of the rotten flesh. You was about to have gangrene—that was what was poisoning you all over—but I think I got it stopped. You might have another bad night or two, but I think you'll be all right before long."

Ed tried to sit up, but Doc Stratton pushed him back. "You're going to have to lay quiet a day or two and let your body mend. You might as well know I've already lost one patient today. Calf broke its back down at Ike Stacy's place south of town. He died in a hurry, and he was in a lot better shape than you are."

Ed managed a lopsided grin, but his thoughts were

not on the doctor's droll humor. He shifted his weight in the bed and drew a sharp breath as pain bit across his back. He shoved his hand under the blanket, searching for his pants pocket, but his Levi's had been removed. He was clad only in his flannel underwear. He glanced anxiously around the room and saw his pants hanging over the back of a chair a few feet away.

"A roll of bills fell out when we yanked your pants off, so I put the money under your pillow, Ed." Matt Latham rose from another chair and walked around to stand beside the bed. "I helped carry you up here from Clayton's, and I came back with the doctor just now to talk some sense to you. Don't kill yourself tryng to pay me and the others a debt you don't owe. Why don't you take Hill's money, ride out, and stay alive?"

Latham's concern for Ed was genuine, but there was more than neighborliness behind his presence here. A place of his own, cattle with his brand on them, a chance to meet the raw challenges of the Texas prairie—these were the rewards which drew men like Matt Latham to the western frontier. While logic and ambition dueled for favor in Latham's mind, he needed to be close to Ed. He could weigh his own desires against the scars on Ed's body and spirit, and come to his own decisions more easily.

Ed asked, "Why don't you ride out and hunt some new land yourself, Matt?"

A sigh shook Latham's heavy shoulders and he looked away. "I reckon I'll have to find another line of work. I'm too old to run off chasing the rainbow anymore, but you'd have some money to get started. You could forget there's a place called Maverick Creek."

Ed's face saddened. "I couldn't, Matt. You wouldn't think much of me if I did."

"No, I reckon not. You've lost more than any of us, and I want to see how you fare from now on, but I feel

144

like a skunk waiting to see what Skillet does to you when you go back while I'm doing nothing."

Ed closed his eyes, feeling that his trip to Singletree had at least not been a complete waste of time. Latham was wrestling with his conscience already, and the other ranchers would be doing the same. "You'll follow me back someday, Matt. I won't worry about being alone too long."

Doc Stratton had ignored the conversation while he fumbled through his medical bag for a bottle of pills. Now he turned back to his patient, waving Matt Latham aside.

"Ain't nobody going to follow you nowhere soon, less'n it's through the Pearly Gates. You've been closer to dead than you know, young feller. Most men would already be dead from fever and shock after what you've been through. If you don't do as I say we still might be singing hymns over you. You keep close to that bed for the next few days."

He put the pills on the washstand next to Ed's bed, gave him instructions for taking them, then walked toward the door. Matt Latham trudged along behind him. Halfway across the room, Matt turned and said, "Ellen Ditmar was up here awhile ago. She's been worried about you. She said she'd look in on you now and then."

Doc Stratton grunted his approval. "That's good. Somebody needs to get hold of me if things don't go right. I don't want you out of this room until your fever is gone, Ed, and you'll need plenty of rest to get rid of it."

There was no argument from Ed. Rest would come a little easier now that he knew where he stood. He had tried his best to get the ranchers to stand together, but the fearful memory of Hill's raid made them reluctant to join him. Both Sheriff Ray Felton and Matt

145

Latham had tried to persuade him to accept Hill's money and ride away. It would be an easy thing to do, but later he would feel like a traitor. He could not forget his promise to Jericho John that he would defend the Triple J as long as he lived, and he could not forget that his father's killer was still free and unpunished. Ed had to stay, regardless of the odds.

His decision meant he was bound to face Brady Wayne again someday. When that time came, he told himself, he wanted to be sure his head was clear and his instincts sharp enough to give him the gun speed he would need.

Chapter Thirteen

For an hour after the doctor left the room with Matt Latham, Ed drifted in and out of a restless sleep. In his feverish mind he heard again the faltering voice of his dying father as they rode on Mescalero Ridge. His mother appeared, her golden hair falling around her shoulders as she tried to make flowers grow around the cabin porch—and he saw a skinny, white-haired little girl peeping shyly at him while she clung to her father's legs.

Suddenly he came fully awake, but he kept his eyes closed, trying to blot out the visions which had populated his dreams. His mother and father were both dead, and Molly had changed so much he was not sure he even knew her anymore. One moment she seemed to care deeply for him; the next moment she seemed just as fond of Brady Wayne.

A suspicion was growing in Ed's mind that Molly had no sincere feeling for either of them, but would choose the one she thought could offer her a life filled with more excitement and adventure. He was beginning to believe she was pitting one against the other just to see what steps they might take to possess her.

After seeing a side of Molly he had not known before, he was not sure she would ever be content at the Triple J, leading the simple life of a ranch wife; but then again there might not be a Triple J for *anyone* to enjoy. The ranch he had hoped to build into a worthwhile heritage would slip away from him forever unless he could win a one-man war against Morgan Hill.

The lamp above his bed had been turned out, and Ed opened his eyes to stare at the darkened ceiling. A murky gray rectangle showed him the location of the single window which opened on the street He rolled over on his side, relieved to find that the wound on his back which Doc Stratton had cauterized was no more painful than before. His skin was hot and dry, however, and he clamped his teeth together to keep them from chattering.

Just as he turned toward the other wall, the door to the hallway swung open and he saw a dark figure framed against the lamplit corridor. Panic froze his stomach for a second, and he lunged toward the gunbelt which Matt Latham had left draped around the post at the foot of the bed.

"You won't need that, Ed."

He recognized Ellen Ditmar's voice and fell limply back on the pillows, breathing hard from the exertion. Ellen came into the room, stopped a moment at the washstand, then lit the lamp. As the light spread around them, Ed saw she had brought a tray with a bowl of soup and a cup of coffee on it.

She sat down on the edge of the bed, her almond brown eyes and jet black hair full of dancing lights. Ed smiled and said, "You gave me a scare, Ellen. I keep wondering who's going to be after me next."

Ellen tossed her hair lightly, and Ed caught a faint aroma which reminded him of lilacs. She still wore the checked apron which was the uniform of the waitresses who worked at the Drover' Pride. The stillness of the rambling hotel told him the dining room was closed now, and that Ellen Ditmar's work was finished for the day.

"I hope I don't scare you every time you see me," she said, smiling. "I think I scared you up on Mescalero Ridge a couple of days ago, talking the way I did about wanting you to notice me."

"You didn't scare me. You just whetted my interest. It took my mind off other things."

"Hmm," she murmured. Her even white teeth flashed a smile. She picked up the coffee cup and handed it to him. "You need to sweat a lot to break up a fever. This might help. I brought some broth, too."

Ed pushed himself to a sitting position, propped his shoulders against the headboard, and lifted the cup to his mouth. His hands shook and he flinched as the hot liquid dribbled down the front of his red flannels. "I know I need to sweat, but I'm freezing all the time."

"It's like an oven in here. You sure shouldn't be cold." A worried frown wrinkled her brow. She closed her hands around his and guided the cup to his lips.

Ed felt embarrassed as she continued to assist him while he spooned down the broth and finished the coffee. Afterward, she gathered the dishes on the tray and started to leave. Ed had slipped back under the blanket and it was rippling from the trembling of his arms and legs.

Ellen's steps slowed and she put the tray down on top of the dresser near the doorway. She turned and looked at him, biting her lip in indecision; then she came back and stood beside the bed.

"When I was a little girl, I had colds and fever al-

149

most every winter. Mother would heat up big round stones she had gathered from the creek, wrap them in towels, and pile them around me until I started sweating. Then the fever would break."

"My folks did the same with me sometimes."

"Well, I don't have any creek stones handy, but you need to be kept warm, Ed. You can't spend the night chilling like this. I'll get you warm."

She loosened the cuffs of her sleeves, kicked off her shoes, and began to unbutton the bodice of her dress. Seeing Ed's eyes on her, she paused and said, "Roll over and turn your back a minute."

He did as he was told, puzzled by her behavior; then she got in the bed with him, drawing the covers up to her shoulders. She pressed against his back, sliding her arm across his waist and drawing him close. She still wore her undergarments, but Ed could feel the firm mounds of her breasts and the roundness of her thighs across his legs.

Caught off-guard by her boldness, Ed lay still for several minutes, afraid to speak. He did not want her to move. He felt a faint stirring of desire, but he was too weak to sustain the sensation. The warmth of her body was comforting and he was sure the chills would soon subside.

Finally he said, "You're a nice girl, Ellen. I'm lucky to have you as a friend."

"I want to be more than a friend, Ed."

Her frankness surprised him, and he fumbled for words. "When I get to feeling better . . . maybe you and I can . . . well, you're already more than a friend — a lot more."

Ed did not know at what point he fell asleep, but his awakening was sudden and unexpected. He heard voices exchanging angry words, and at first he thought they were somewhere along the hallway; then he realized the sounds were in his own room.

As he opened his eyes, coming quickly alert, he was first conscious of the dampness surrounding him. The mattress beneath him was soggy and his red flannels were clinging to him, soaked with perspiration. Apparently Ellen had drawn away from him after his fever broke. She was on the far edge of the bed, sitting erect with her hands clutching the covers under her chin. Five feet away, at the foot of the bed, stood Lonnie Grayson. His legs were spread wide in a belligerent stance. His hands were on his hips, and his handsome face was fiery red.

Ellen was saying, "I told you to get out of here and leave us alone, Lonnie. Give me time to get dressed and I'll come downstairs and explain."

"Explain?" A forced laugh rattled in Lonnie Grayson's throat. "You don't need to explain, Ellen. Any fool can see what's been going on."

"Nothing's been going on," Ellen said, exasperated. "I don't have to explain anything to you."

Ed sat up in bed, bracing his back against the headboard. The lamp was still flickering above him, but it wasn't needed. The night had passed, and Ed saw the gray and pink of dawn reflected in the window. From the second floor of the hotel he could see the opposite side of the street, and people were already beginning to move about.

As Lonnie Grayson took a step toward Ellen, Ed asked sharply, "What are you doing in my room?"

Lonnie whirled to look at Ed Jessup. His lower lip quivered and he ran his fingers along the holster which held his notched gun.

"I was looking for Ellen," he snarled. "I was going to ride out for a look around our ranch this morning,

151

and I came over here to ask her to go along. She wasn't in her room, so I asked the old lady who runs the place if she'd seen her. She told me the last she saw of her was when she was bringing food up to you last night. I knocked on your door twice, but I guess both of you was too tired to answer. It was unlocked, so I came on in—and look what I found—you and my girl in bed together!"

"Now, look here, Lonnie—" Ed began.

"Your girl?" Ellen cut in indignantly. "I'm not your girl, Lonnie, and I never have been."

"That's not true," Lonnie waved his arms. "You were my girl when I left five years ago, and you acted like you were still my girl when I got back here."

Ellen tossed her hair and wadded the covers tighter in her fists. "I went around with you some, Lonnie, and maybe I let you kiss me once or twice, but that was a long time ago, and people change. I don't belong to you. I'll make up my own mind who's girl I am."

"It's Jessup's fault!" Lonnie raged. He rubbed his hand across the gun butt again, his finger tracing the thin notch there. "I'm a good mind to blow your head off, Jessup, but your gun is out of reach, so I've got an idea that'll work just as well. I'm going over to Clayton's and tell Sam Ditmar what happened up here last night. He'll come after you with a shotgun."

Ed pulled away from the headboard and squared his shoulders. He had regained some strength and it showed in the way he sat, poised, as if to spring toward the man at the foot of the bed. "Texas folk don't take kindly to anybody who bad-mouths a good woman, Lonnie. You ought to know that. You go spreading lies about Ellen, and Sam Ditmar's more likely to shoot you than me. If that ain't enough to keep you quiet, I'll personally kick in your face as soon as I'm able to stand on my own two feet. Ellen has told the truth. She stayed here to help me get rid of the fever, and I think it worked. That's all that happened. Believe that, Lonnie, and let's try to get along. Let's fight Skillet, not each other."

For several seconds Lonnie stared at Ed, his body shaking with anger. Then he turned and stalked toward the door. Over his shoulder, he said, "I'll fight Skillet, all right, but I'm not through with you, Jessup. I'll settle with you later."

Lonnie's intrusion was unsettling, and silence hung over the room for a while after he left. Finally Ellen said, "It's time for the breakfast trade. I've got to go to work. I've got just about enough time to go to my room and freshen up a little before I go downstairs. I really didn't think I'd sleep through the whole night, but I did."

As she had before, she asked Ed to turn away while she dressed. Afterward, she told him she would send the handyman up with warm water to fill the big tin tub in the corner of the room so he could have a bath.

"Matt Latham put your bedroll under the bed," she told him, "and I suppose you have some fresh flannels in it. When I'm through working tonight I'll wash up those things you're wearing now." She bent across the bed, touched her lips lightly to his, and smiled. "You sure changed a lot overnight, Ed. I guess you're not going to die after all."

"That was never in my plans." Ed grinned and watched appreciatively as her trim figure disappeared through the doorway.

He spent the remainder of the week at the Drover's

Pride, wanting to be sure he was completely well before he left town. Each day he grew stronger, but more restless. He was eager to get back to his land and start rebuilding the Triple J.

Doc Stratton checked on him the first two days, then expressed satisfaction with his progress and did not come again. Louella Vance, the plump, matronly widow who had inherited the hotel when her husband died, visited him occasionally to help him pass the time with conversation.

It was Ellen Ditmar's company which made the idle days bearable, however. She continued to bring his meals to the room, often carrying a tray for herself so he would not have to eat alone. They talked of their youth, and of the troubles which Morgan Hill and the Skillet crew had heaped upon the ranchers who lived on Maverick Creek.

Ellen was a lively, interesting companion — a woman who could be extremely serious one moment and full of wit and humor the next. They were completely at ease with each other, and Ed found himself liking her more each time he saw her.

Ellen made no attempt to talk Ed out of his decision to fight for his land. In fact, she seemed more incensed by the loss of her home than most of the men who had been driven away by Skillet.

"I hate working here for room and board and two dollars a week," she told him one day. "We had a chance to be somebody, and I want my mother and father to have something of their own before they die. My father will go back with you, Ed — I'll shame him into it if I have to."

"He could get killed," Ed said. "I'm sure Skillet will hit us again if we move back. Morgan Hill has decided what he wants, and he's too used to having his own way to back down. I think Sam Ditmar knows that."

She studied his face. The bruises from Brady Wayne's fists and the marks from the dragging incident had healed and disappeared. He had shaved the stubble from his bronzed face and his pale blue eyes were clear again. Ellen sat admiring the rugged good looks which had always attracted her to him.

"Something tells me you want Skillet to come again," she said. "I think you want a fight."

Ed's response was immediate. "I guess I do. It's got to be settled, and the sooner the better. I want somebody to pay for what happened to my pa and for what Skillet has done to us all, but I want to stay clear of the law and the sheriff. Ray Felton hinted that he won't take a hand if Skillet makes a move on my own land. Yeah, I want Skillet to come to me. This time I'll be ready."

After the conversation, Ellen left the room looking reassured.

During his stay at the hotel Ed did not see Lonnie Grayson again, but it was not long before he heard disturbing news about him. Four days after he collapsed in the back room of Clayton's Saloon, Ed took breakfast in the Drover's Pride dining room for the first time. Ellen was there, bustling about and smiling pleasantly at the people waiting to catch the stage and the half dozen customers who made a daily ritual of taking their morning meal at the hotel. She greeted Ed and gave him a seat at a table near the front window.

The sun was barely above the eastern horizon, sending fanlike shafts of color into the dawn sky, but people and horses were already moving along Main Street. Sam Ditmar came by the window on his way to his job at the saloon. He caught a glimpse of Ed Jessup, turned, and came inside. He looked pleased as he seated himself at Ed's table.

"Son of a gun!" He laughed and reached across to slap Ed's arm. "It's good to see you up and about, son. Me and Harve and the rest of us thought it best to leave you alone until you got well; that's why we didn't visit none, but Ellen has been keeping tabs on you, and she's kept me up-to-date. How are you feeling?"

"Mean and aggravated," Ed said. "Like myself again. I'm going to spend the day buying up some things I need, then tomorrow I'm going back to Maverick Creek."

"What do you think Skillet will do?"

"They'll watch me for a while, and try to figure out if I'm just there to gather up the stuff that's left. When they see I'm building a house and mean to stay, they'll come after me. I won't be inside a cabin where they can find me the next time. During the day I can see them coming, and every night I'll hide out in a different place. If Hill's men come on my land I aim to pick them off just like a bushwhacker would."

Seeing her father at the table, Ellen came over and rubbed her hand through his thinning hair. She inquired about her mother, kissed her father on the cheek, then hurried away. Presently she returned to bring a platter of steak and eggs for Ed, and an extra cup of coffee for her father.

Sam Ditmar waited until Ellen walked away, then turned his head to be sure she was beyond the sound of his voice. He said, "You need to talk some sense into Lonnie Grayson. He's trying to get up men for a raid on Skillet. He keeps egging on the cowboys who used to ride for us and wants them to back him up. Folks say he's been calling you all kinds of sorry names. What did you do to make him so mad?"

"Nothing," Ed said quickly. His face colored and he ducked closer to his plate, hoping Sam Ditmar would not notice that the question caused him a moment of anxiety. Apparently Lonnie Grayson had heeded Ed's warning and had not told anyone about seeing Ellen in Ed Jessup's bed. "I haven't done anything to Lonnie that I know of."

"He's a wild one," Sam Ditmar grunted. "He could make things worse."

Ed sipped his coffee. "Lonnie just needs to grow up. He's almost as old as I am, but he acts like a kid. He's a show-off and likes to get attention. Those cowboys won't follow Lonnie. They've got better sense. Don't worry about it, Sam."

Sam Ditmar had little more to say before he finished his coffee and left. Ed watched him along the street and saw the slump of his shoulders and the sluggishness of his steps. He was a cowman who liked the odor of grass and sage and the heat of the sun on his face. It was clear he did not relish the prospect of spending another day as a saloon man's helper.

When he finished his breakfast, Ed waved to Ellen and went into the gloomy, boxlike lobby which adjoined the dining room. He waited on one of the wooden benches along the wall while a whiskey drummer in a stained salt-and-pepper suit settled his account, then paid his bill.

Louella Vance cooed and chuckled and complimented him on his refreshed appearance. She charged him only half the usual rate, excusing the difference by saying he had caused her only half as much work since Ellen had cared for both him and

157

his room. He paid for an extra night's lodging, explaining that he would be leaving before sunrise the next day.

Word of Jericho John Jessup's death had spread through the town and across the range. As Ed moved from place to place to do his shopping, people stopped him to express their regrets. Many of them were strangers, but they had heard of Jericho John.

Ed spent most of the day rounding up his needs. He bought bacon, canned goods, tar paper, nails, and a new pair of Levi's at Lance Barker's General Store. At the Cattleman's Outfitters Store on the edge of town, he found an iron cookstove, a bed frame and mattress, two sheets of glass, and some logging chain. At both places he arranged to have the merchandise stacked near the door so he could pick it up early the next morning.

In late afternoon he visited McPherson's Livery to check on his horse and to rent a team of mules and a buckboard to haul his supplies to the ranch. Adam McPherson was glad to see him, and after they had finished their business, he insisted that Ed sit and talk for a spell.

Ed had always enjoyed the company of the rotund, good-natured liveryman and welcomed a chance to relax for a few minutes. McPherson wanted to hear firsthand the details of the Skillet raid which had led to John Jessup's death. Ed gave him a brief account of events from the time Morgan Hill's men had dragged him across the prairie at the end of a rope until he collapsed in the back room of Clayton's Saloon.

While he talked, Ed ran his glance over the walls of McPherson's stuffy little office. It was a fascinating place to while away the time. McPherson was an avid reader and a dedicated collector. The office walls were covered with newspaper clippings, old "Wanted" fliers, reproductions of tintypes cut from newspapers and magazines, imprints of the many branding irons he had fashioned over the years, Comanche arrowheads, and strings of Indian beads. Over the years, Ed had spent many hours looking into the grim faces of robbers, rustlers, and killers who glared back at him from those walls.

Noticing his interest, McPherson rose from his chair and jabbed a finger at a fresh newspaper clipping. "This here's a story about your pa's death. I wrote up some notes and gave them to the stage driver to pass on at the junction for a relay to the *Galveston News*. I write up stuff for them once in awhile, and they pay me a few dollars a year. I didn't have much to go on—just what Ellen Ditmar told me after she ran into you on Mescalero Ridge. They filled in Jericho John's background. They had it in their files, I reckon."

Ed stood beside McPherson and read the story. The headline said: FAMED FAST GUN DEAD IN SINGLE-TREE. It was a lengthy article, but most of it was devoted to a review of Jericho John Jessup's exploits during his early years.

Lacking information, McPherson had been careful in the way he phrased the report of the rancher's death. The story said only that Jericho John had died of a gunshot wound as a result of a difficulty with a neighboring ranch. It did not mention Skillet or Morgan Hill's name.

"Pa would have liked that," Ed said, returning to his seat. "He liked to see his name in the papers."

McPherson nodded, then changed the subject. "Hear you've been buying a lot of stuff. Flashing a lot

159

of money around."

Ed was annoyed that his activities had become the subject of gossip. "Folks ought to mind their own business," he said.

"You'd never guess who mentioned it." McPherson did not wait for Ed to comment. "It was one of the Skillet riders. They're coming and going all the time. One of them said he saw you at the Cattleman's Outfitters. He told me about it when he came by to pick up his horse."

Shrugging, Ed reached into his Levi's pocket and took out his money. He fanned the bank notes in his hand, brushing absently at the bloodstains which marked the edge of them.

"It's the money I was going to buy breed stock with," he told the liveryman, "but I'm using it up to start over again. I've got two hundred and eighty dollars left. If you have any contact with that cattle dealer, Wally Ogden, tell him I'll take whatever stockers this will buy. I'm still going to put some Herefords on Triple J some day."

McPherson's face clouded. "It's my notion the Skillet man told me about seeing you just because he knows I'm a friend of yours. He wants you to know they're watching you. The minute I heard you were buying supplies, I knew you meant to hang tough on Maverick Creek. I'm worried, Ed."

Ed stood up to leave. "I'm worried, too, Adam," he said, and started walking slowly back to the hotel.

Chapter Fourteen

A thin sheet of smoky clouds slid in from the northwest, turning the Texas sky slate gray. Dusk came early to Singletree. Ed Jessup had grown so familiar with the sparse furnishings of his hotel room he did not bother to light the lamp while he gathered his belongings, packed his gear, and prepared for his early morning departure.

He saw Ellen Ditmar only briefly when he went down to the dining room for supper. She served him a meal of steak, potatoes, and stewed tomatoes, and stood near his shoulder while he told her how he had spent the day. She was going to leave the hotel early this evening, she said, because she had promised to meet her mother at Myrtle Cooper's house, then go with the two of them to evening church service.

When Ed stood up to leave, she came back to the table, squeezed his hand, and said softly, "I may never see you again, Ed. I'd like to have a long, long kiss right now."

She was close to him, her lips only a few inches from his. Ed felt his skin tingle as blood rushed to his face. He leaned away from her and glanced uncomfortably around the room to see if the half dozen other diners were watching them.

161

"Not here, Ellen."

Ellen Dimar laughed. "Don't look so flustered. I'm not going to do it—I just said I'd like to." Her expression became solemn, her dark eyes holding his glance. "After all these years, I feel like I've finally got to know you, Ed. Don't get yourself killed and leave me now. Be careful."

Ed touched her shoulder. "You'll see me again," he said, and hurried away.

Back in his room, Ed paced the floor. He stopped in front of the window, studying the cloudy sky. Rain would be good for the rangeland, but the clouds were too high and moving too swiftly to offer much hope. It was just as well, he thought, if it remained dry. Good weather would give him a chance to check on his cattle and cut some small timber from the ridge to build a new cabin.

Moving away from the window, he sat on the edge of the bed and tugged off his boots. His stomach muscles were tight. Fear and apprehension were working on his nerves and there was a knot of doubt inside him. While making his rounds during the day, he had seen Matt Latham at Barker's store and Harve Grayson at McPherson's Livery. Each had shaken hands with him, passed a few remarks, then busied himself with chores. The way they fidgeted and avoided looking at him told Ed they were ashamed of their own fears—afraid they might appear cowardly because they had declined to join him. He had heard nothing new from Sam Ditmar despite Ellen's determination to persuade her father to return to Maverick Creek.

Ed was disappointed, but not offended by their attitude. He had started this trouble, and somehow he

162

would have to finish it. For a while he sat staring at the floor, pondering the odds against him, but he had no thought of giving up. He blew out the lamp, undressed, and stretched out on the bed, figuring this would be the last good night's rest he would enjoy in a long time.

As it turned out, it was one of the worst nights of his life. He woke up suddenly with the eerie awareness that he was not alone in the room. He did not know what time it was, but there were no sounds from the street and the room was so dark he could not see the walls. The fine hairs on the back of his neck crinkled and a clammy sweat broke out across his forehead.

Before he could move, there was a flurry of motion at his back. The covers were yanked over his head, stifling his breath. Quickly a length of rope circled the covers, drawing tightly around his neck, and forming a hood over his head. Strong hands continued to loop the rope around him, pinning his arms so he was helpless.

"We want the money, mister," a muffled voice said. "We know you've got a roll of bills with you. Tell us where you've stashed it or I'll bend this gun barrel around your head and search until we find it. Save yourself a big headache and tell us where it is."

A sinking sensation lodged in Ed's stomach, but he obeyed. If he were knocked unconscious, the money was going to be lost anyway, and he did not want to waste more time under a doctor's care. He said, "It's in my pocket—in those Levi's hanging on the chair over there."

The bed vibrated as someone bumped against it in the darkness. Spurs rattled and booted feet scuffed against the floor. He heard a man's voice grunt in triumph, then the opening and closing of the door to the hallway. The only sound left in the room was his own heavy breathing inside the hood.

The rope around him had not been knotted. It was meant to restrain him only long enough for him to give up or be knocked unconscious. Ed freed himself in a matter of minutes.

When he lighted the lamp, he saw his Levi's lying on the floor, the pockets turned inside out, and he knew he was now penniless except for the two silver dollars he had poked into the toe of each of his boots. He was glad he had already paid for his supplies, but was saddened by the thought of how long and hard he and his father had worked for the money.

For a while Ed sat in the chair, his elbows on his knees, his head resting in his hands. He had no idea who had stolen his money, but he knew it was a lone man. The thief had kept saying "we" and "us", but that was an attempt to mislead him. There had been only one set of footsteps and only one person had left the room.

Did Skillet have a hand in it? Leaving him broke would serve two purposes for Morgan Hill. It might keep Ed from buying everything he needed to rebuild his home, and, perhaps, encourage him to take Hill's money and sign a quit-claim.

McPherson had told him a Skillet rider had mentioned seeing Ed with a roll of money, but anyone with more than a few dollars in his hands was bound to attract attention in a town like Singletree. By now, dozens of people knew he had been carrying a sizable sum. There had been other customers at the stores he had visited. Ellen Ditmar knew about the money, and so did Matt Latham, Harve Grayson, and Adam McPherson.

He could not be sure about the Skillet crew, but he pushed aside any thought that Morgan Hill might be involved. The Skillet owner was tough and vengeful, but he was too proud to engage in petty thievery.

There was no point in trying to pursue the robber. The Drover's Pride had entrances from the side, the rear, and the front, and they were seldom locked. A man could come and go in the dead of night without notice, and a thief would not be foolish enough to linger long at the scene of his crime.

Ed crossed the room and took tobacco and papers from his shirt pocket. He smoked a cigarette to settle his nerves, then went back to sleep. The loss of the money would not change his plans.

At dawn Ed left the hotel, his bedroll slung across one shoulder. He walked to the livery stable to get the buckboard and his horse. McPherson and Harve Grayson already had the mules hitched to the wagon. Ed rubbed the buckskin's nose and tied it with a lead rope at the rear of the buckboard.

He saw no reason to tell them about the robbery. When he started to leave, Harve Grayson put an arm across his shoulder and said, "Good luck, Ed," and walked toward the stalls, his head down.

After he had picked up his supplies, Ed brought the wagon back along Main Street. Loading the wagon had taken longer than he expected, and the sun was already well above the horizon. The slanting rays were hot against his face, warning of a blistering day to come. The clouds of the night before had drifted away, and it would be weeks before another hint of rain.

Bringing the buckboard to a halt by the rail in front of the town jail, Ed sat a moment staring at the doorway to Marshal Dan Plover's office. He set the brake handle, looped the reins around it, and stepped to the boardwalk. Although he had little confidence in Plover's ability to help, Ed had decided to tell the marshal about being robbed of his money. He found the jail door locked. After shaking it several times, he walked on to Clayton's Saloon.

He had planned to cook his own breakfast somewhere along the trail to Maverick Creek, but time had slipped away and he was hungry. In addition to spirits, Hal Clayton provided a few food items for his regular customers. Townsmen who could not afford the fare at the Drover's Pride often started their day with a snack at the saloon.

Ed stopped just inside the door to adjust his eyes to the gloom and to have a look around. Marshal Dan Plover stood with an elbow next to the glass jar which held the pickled eggs. He had a slab of cheese in one hand, a piece of bread in the other, and a mug of beer in front of him. At a table near the end of the bar Ed saw Harve Grayson and Adam McPherson.

He passed along the front of the bar on his way to speak to the marshal, and a hand touched his sleeve. He looked around at Hal Clayton, a wiry, red-haired man with freckles scattered over his face. The saloon man gestured with his thumb and said in a husky whisper, "Feller over there came in early. He's been asking about you and watching the street. He said he needed to see you before you left town."

Ed put his back against the bar and looked toward the far wall. That side of the room was in shadow, and he had not seen the man seated at the table there with a half-empty glass and a bottle of whiskey in front of him.

"Drinking hard stuff kind of early," Ed murmured.

"Drinking mean, too, I think," Clayton said, his voice low. "I've never seen him before, but I don't like his looks."

Seeing their eyes on him, the man lifted his head. He pushed back a dusty black Stetson and met their glance with an emotionless stare. He was a little man. Ed guessed he was no more than five feet tall. His face was long. His pointed chin jutted out so that his mouth looked like a notch cut into wood.

Ed scowled and lowered his hand along his right thigh. He lifted his Colt up and down by the trigger guard to be sure it was loose in the holster. "I know that face," he told Clayton. "I saw it on a flier over at McPherson's."

"Is he an outlaw?"

"You might say so. He hires out his gun to whoever will pay for it, and he doesn't care how he gets the job done."

Adam McPherson, spotting Ed talking with Clayton, scooted along the counter to join them. His eyes were wide and sweat lay in the folds of his neck. "You know who that man over by the wall is, Ed? I've got an old wanted—"

"I know who it is, Adam. It's Milo Sloan. That poster of yours says the sheriff down in Duval County will pay two hundred and fifty dollars to anybody who brings him in. He shot two or three people around there, one of them in the back, as I recall."

McPherson wiped his chin, shielding his mouth as he whispered, "Hope he didn't hear us talking. What does he want with you?"

During the conversation they had turned their backs to the man at the table, but Ed could still feel Milo Sloan's gaze on him. A shiver of dread ran along his spine. "I don't know, Adam, and I'm not going to take time to find out. I've got things to do. I should have been halfway home by now."

"You hombres talkin' about me?"

Milo Sloan stood up and strode to the center of the room. His batwing chaps were scarred and discolored, indicating he had ridden often through the brush of unmarked trails, the kind of terrain a man on the dodge would choose. The ivory butt of the big .44 Colt on his thigh was worn smooth and it was yellowed with age.

Ed answered, "Yeah, we were talking about you — just the natural curiosity folks hereabouts have about strangers. No harm was meant."

McPherson backed away from Ed, going to stand beside Marshal Dan Plover. Hal Clayton walked to the other end of the bar and busied himself polishing glasses.

"Curiosity killed the cat," Milo Sloan said, laughing dryly. His voice was a nasal drawl. He took another step forward and planted his stubby legs wide part. His right hand hovered above the low-slung gun. "You want to get yourself killed, too?"

Ed shrugged and looked toward the town marshal. Dan Plover was still eating. He had his back half-turned and was ignoring the exchange at the center of the room. Ed started toward him, but Milo Sloan's voice stopped him.

"Are you Ed Jessup?" Sloan asked. When Ed nodded, the man said, "I thought so. I was over in Mesa

Springs when the stage driver left off a newspaper. It had a story in it about your old man gettin' himself killed. I've been lookin' for Jericho John Jessup for years. Now that somebody beat me to him, you'll have to pay his debt."

Instinct told Ed where the conversation was leading. He felt his pulse racing. "What kind of debt?"

"A blood debt." Milo Sloan's voice was threatening. "Jericho John Jessup was a yellow-bellied, back-shootin' bounty hunter. He killed my brother over Four Corners way. He claimed he was rustlin' and shot him in the back. Family blood is family blood. My brother's gone, your pa's gone, and that leaves it between you and me."

"You talk like a crazy man, mister." Ed's voice was harsh. "Watch your mouth when you talk about my pa. He told me about every man he ever shot. There was nobody named Sloan. He never worked around Four Corners and he never shot anybody in the back."

"You're a liar, Jessup!" Milo Sloan's lids drooped, shading his watery gray eyes. "Your pa was a lily-livered coward and a bushwhacker. That newspaper piece said he left behind one son — you. I rode like hell to get in here last night, and I've been waitin' ever since to tell you what kind of skunk your old man was. You're goin' to pay his debt — you've got no choice. I aim to kill you right here and now."

Ed took a step away from the bar and braced his legs in a way that put his gun at a handy angle. He looked cautiously toward Dan Plover. "Milo Sloan is a wanted man, marshal. He's a back-shooter and a gun for hire by anybody who pays. There's a reward out on him. You ought to take him in."

Marshal Plover whirled around as though he had just noticed something unusual was going on. Bread crumbs clung to the stubble on his chin. His voice quavering, he said, "Now, lookee here, Ed, I know who he is. I recollect his face from one of them old fliers I passed on to McPherson, but what he done was miles from here. I got no jurisdiction over that. He ain't broke no laws in Singletree that I know of. I can't arrest a man for just talking."

Milo Sloan laughed, but it had a forced sound. Tension turned his face haggard and gray. The thin strands of oily hair which hung down from his hatband were almost white. He was older than Ed had first judged him to be—probably in his sixties. Sloan said, "You're goin' to keep after the marshal till he gets so scared he'll throw up all over the place. He don't want no truck with me. He ain't goin' to help you, Jessup."

Ed wanted to spit at Marshal Dan Plover to show his disdain for the man's weakness, but his throat was too dry to accommodate him. He looked squarely at Milo Sloan. "You've cooked up a tale just to start a fight. The marshal ain't going to arrest you, and I don't much care about you. You're an old man, too old to be acting tough anymore. If you want to get any older, you'll find your horse and ride out of Singletree. You'll be a dead man if you make me draw on you."

Sloan cocked his head. "They tell me Jericho John was the fastest gun there was in his time. You can't be that good, sonny."

"I'm better," Ed said. "He told me so himself."

"We'll see." Sloan's bony shoulders stiffened. He tucked his sharp chin closer to his neck. "I don't do

170

no countin' or give no warnin's, Jessup. I just draw and shoot, and that's when you'll—"

While he was still talking, Milo Sloan's hand swept downward to the big .44 Colt. An ear-shattering explosion boomed through the room, reverberating against the walls, and Sloan's reedy voice ceased to be heard.

There might have been a time when Milo Sloan's gun hand moved with blinding speed, but that time had passed. He had got his gun clear of its holster, but he was never able to lift it into firing position. It was still pointing toward the floor when the bullet from Ed Jessup's gun ripped through Sloan's cheekbone and tore his face apart. Sloan turned half around, then crashed to the floor face down. His legs thrashed in the sawdust a few times, then grew still. Milo Sloan was dead.

Ed stared wide-eyed at the smoking gun in his own hand, stunned by the ease and swiftness with which he had drawn and fired. His hand started to shake, and he quickly holstered the gun, folding his arms across his chest to calm his nerves.

The gunshot startled Marshal Dan Plover and he spilled beer down his shirtfront. He moved away from the bar, brushing at the dampness around his belt buckle. Harve Grayson made a choking sound in his throat and Adam McPherson swore under his breath. Sam Ditmar rushed out of the back room, wringing an apron. "My God, you've killed him."

Hal Clayton hurried from behind the bar, pushing Sam Ditmar aside. They gathered in a semicircle around the silent form on the floor. The marshal knelt beside the body. "We'd best see if he's got some papers or something on him to make sure he's Milo

Sloan."

Rummaging through the man's Levi's, Dan Plover laid aside a spare cinch ring, a two-bit piece, two horseshoe nails, and a wad of rope about the length of a pigging string. He ran his fingers inside the pockets of Sloan's hide vest and pulled out some folded bank notes. He smoothed the money in the palm of his hand and counted it. "He was carrying a hundred dollars," the marshal said.

Ed Jessup stared at the money. He leaned over for a closer look at the bills and saw the rusty stain along the edges of them. "That's my money, marshal. Somebody busted into my room last night, hung me up in the covers, and took all I had. That's what I came in here to tell you when I got into it with Sloan. There's still a hundred and eighty dollars missing. When you find the man who's got the rest of those bloodstained bills, we'll know who robbed me and who hired Milo Sloan to kill me."

"I'll keep a lookout," the marshal said, rising. He extended the hand with the money in it. "I guess you'll be wanting this back."

Ed took the money from the marshal's hand and shoved it into his pocket. "Now I know what somebody thinks my life is worth—a hundred dollars."

"Some say it won't be worth a plugged nickel if you don't make a deal with Skillet," Sam Ditmar said.

"Then Skillet better be on the lookout for a plugged nickel," Ed replied. "I'm heading for Maverick Creek right now."

He looked again at the torn, bloody face of the dead man on the floor. His stomach fluttered with nausea. He had never killed a man, and the victory over Milo Sloan gave him no sense of triumph. The finality of it was just beginning to seep into his mind, and he felt sick. He shook his head from side to side, then turned and went out the door.

Chapter Fifteen

Work on the new cabin occupied most of Ed Jessup's time for the next three weeks. It took him two days to clear away the rubble of the old cabin, then he went into the hills to find suitable timber. Trees were not plentiful in this area, and most of the logs had to be cut from the post oaks and pines on Mescalero Ridge.

Although he was accustomed to hard work, the crosscut saw and double-bitted ax called upon muscles Ed did not use every day. His hands were raw with blisters at first, but they soon turned to hard calluses. He worked from dawn to dark every day. At night he ached with fatigue and soreness. All the time he kept a lookout for any sign that Skillet might try to stop him.

Some nights he slept in the barn, and at other times far out on the prairie, or somewhere on Mescalero Ridge amid the logs and bark trimmings he had piled up. He kept the mules he had rented from McPherson and used them to drag the logs to the cabin site. With the chains he had bought at the Cattleman's Outfitters he was able to bind them together so the mules could pull them out four or five at a time.

The cabin was to be a symbol — visible evidence that Ed had not abandoned his ranch — but it was not his only concern. At least twice a week he spent a half day riding around the range, checking on his cattle. His uneasiness about the risk he was taking increased, however, after one of his trips to the section near Maverick Creek where he and his father had bunched the steers they hoped to sell. The cattle had drifted apart, and he circled them, trying to haze them back into a small herd which would continue to graze together.

Remembering their last day's work together, Ed felt a painful longing for his father's company whenever he came here. On this day, his sadness made him lonely and listless, and he began to have second thoughts about his ability to hold out against Morgan Hill. It was almost dark by the time he finished working with the cattle, and he was too tired to do any more riding. He decided to camp where he was.

Since he moved his sleeping place often, Ed carried his bedroll behind his saddle most of the time, and he wasted little time spreading it out for the night. He did not build a fire, but ate a cold supper from the supply of jerky and corn dodgers he kept wrapped in an oilskin along with his blankets. He fell asleep almost as soon as he lay down.

In the middle of the night, Ed awoke with a start, unnerved by a creepy feeling that he was not alone. He sat up and swung his glance around, looking for any sign of an intruder. The moon was down, but the starlit sky was bright enough to give him a good view of his immediate surroundings. Nothing within his sight was moving, and all he could hear were the sounds of cattle munching grass nearby and the rippling current of the creek farther to his left.

Ed reached for his gun, which he had left beside his saddle, and stood up. He walked away a few paces, then stopped, squinting his eyes on a far-off speck of light he had missed before. Ed swore softly under his breath.

Quickly, he gathered up his belongings. He unhobbled his horse, saddled it, and rode toward the light. When he topped a small knoll a few minutes later, he could see a reddish halo hanging in the air above the light, and said aloud, "That's a campfire. Somebody's prowling where they've got no business."

Ed estimated that the fire was about a mile away, somewhere west of his cabin, and he headed in that direction. He lost sight of it after half an hour, and began circling back and forth, scanning the dark land for some sign that would lead him to it. Finally, looking down from the rim of a dry wash, he saw a wisp of smoke rising from the ground. He eased his horse down the shallow bank and found what was left of the campfire.

It had been built between two rows of small rocks. A few embers still glowed on one stick of wood, sending up a curl of smoke. There was a clump of coffee grounds atop the ashes where someone had dumped the contents of the pot to douse the fire. Whoever had been there apparently had seen or heard Ed coming and had made a hurried departure.

Dismounting, he walked around the campsite for a few minutes, studying the tracks of a man's boots and a shod horse, but it was too dark to determine which way the camper had gone. Sighing, Ed hobbled his horse again, tossing the saddle and bedroll on the ground a few feet from the dead campfire. He stretched out with his head propped against the bedroll and went to sleep, feeling confident that the camper would not risk returning to the spot.

At dawn, as Ed rode away from the dry wash, he felt less concerned about the unknown camper. The fire might have belonged to a drifter, he told himself, riding through the area looking for a job. But later, when he found the tracks of a horse in the soft soil around his cabin, his suspicions returned. Frowning, his pulse suddenly pounding in his ears, Ed said to himself, "Skillet's keeping an eye on me."

Stepping out of the saddle for a closer look, Ed followed the horseshoe prints around the cabin site. He soon determined that they led away from the ranch yard toward the gully where he had found the campfire. He gazed around in all directions, wondering if he was still being watched, then shrugged and led his horse to the corral. He had too much work to do to worry about things which might or might not mean something.

By the end of the second week, Ed had enough material at the cabin site to begin actual construction. Using the remaining stone chimney as a starting point, he laid out the foundation logs in a rectangle around it. He notched the corners carefully, making sure each timber fitted closely so that little chinking would be required. It was tiring work and progress was slow. After three days he had only four tiers in place, and the work became more difficult. As the walls grew in height, he had trouble keeping one end of a log in place while he tried to lift the other.

Despite his determination to build the house, he was not sure he could do it alone. He was just about to give up when help came unexpectedly. It was late afternoon, and Ed was sitting in the sparse shade of the dying pecan tree, surveying with disappointment the one row of timbers he had managed to add to the walls during a full day's work. He heard a horse coming up behind him.

His rifle was propped against the chimney and Ed ran toward it without taking time to look around. When he turned, he set the gun down and relaxed. The rider was a hundred yards away, but Ed recognized the slim frame of Sam Ditmar.

Minutes later, Ditmar reined his horse in beneath the tree and stepped down with a grin. Ed grasped his hand. "You're a sight for sore eyes, Sam. It's so lonesome out here I was beginning to talk to myself."

"I'm here for more than a howdy-do," Ditmar said. "I'm here to help."

"Are you sure you've got time, Sam?"

"I aim to take time. We had a meeting in town last night—me and Harve Grayson, Matt Latham, and Clay Siler. We're all going to help. One of us will take a day off every four days. That won't hurt our pay much. It's about a four-hour ride, but that gives us six or seven hours before we head back for the night." He eyed the outline of the cabin. You ain't done bad by yourself, Ed."

"It's been slow."

"It'll go faster now . . . and don't feel obligated. You're going to pay us back. We'll get your cabin up and see what happens. If Skillet leaves you alone, we're all going to build back. We'll expect you to swap work with us."

Ed chuckled. "Fair enough. That's the best news I've heard in a long spell."

A log at a time, a day at a time, the cabin walls grew in height. Extra hands pushed the work along.

Sam Ditmar, Matt Latham, and Clay Siler worked steadily, wasting little time with idle talk. They were hard-muscled, strong, and skilled in the use of tools. By the time Harve Grayson arrived for his turn on the job, the walls were head high and the doors and windows were framed.

Ed was in a good mood throughout the week. Staying busy, and having someone to keep him company, helped relieve his grief over his father's death. But Harve Grayson brought enough worries with him to dampen Ed's spirits.

"I'm worried about that boy of mine," Grayson said shortly after greeting Ed. "Lonnie is still spoiling for a fight. He thinks we ought to be shooting up Skillet instead of building cabins. I can't do nothing with him — never could. He rode out this way yesterday. He said he was going to look around our place. Have you seen anything of him?"

Ed shook his head. Harve Grayson dismounted, hobbled his roan in a patch of grass nearby, picked up an ax, and started notching a log. "Looks like you'll be ready to put this place under a roof next week." He held the ax still a moment and said heavily, "I hope Lonnie don't get himself killed trying to start something with Morgan Hill's outfit."

"Lonnie won't have to worry about getting a chance to fight," Ed said. He swung his gaze southward in the direction of the Skillet Ranch. "If he plans to throw in with me, he'll get all the fighting he wants. Morgan will be coming after me sooner or later."

Harve Grayson's eyes followed Ed's gaze. He stood that way a moment, then began swinging the ax with a vigor which reflected the anger he felt.

"Tomorrow's Sunday, and we'll be taking the day

off," Ed said. "I'll see if I can find Lonnie and calm him down. I don't want us to get blamed for starting a range war. I want that to fall on Morgan Hill's back."

Shortly after sunrise the next day Ed went out to find Lonnie Grayson. To the rest of the world it might have been a quiet and peaceful Sunday morning, but Ed rode with a sense of foreboding. Sheriff Ray Felton had warned him not to fire the first shot in a range war, and he had accepted that advice seriously. He could not hold on to his ranch from a jail cell, and he did not intend to let some impulsive action by Lonnie Grayson put him in one.

He saw the horse first, a glistening black mustang with its forelegs stiffened, its rear sloping downward in the way a cutting horse uses its weight to hold a roped steer in check. A taut line stretched away from the saddle horn, but the other end of the rope was hidden from Ed's sight by a clump of brush.

Circling the buckskin, Ed soon had Lonnie Grayson in view. Lonnie was hovering over a tied-down steer. He had a knee wedged against the animal's ribs, one hand grasping its muzzle and stretching its neck forward. In the other hand, Lonnie held a long-bladed skinning knife poised above the steer's throat. The rangeland way of butchering beef was to slit the neck from ear to ear, drawing out the blood so the meat would be clean and pure.

Lonnie heard the scraping of hooves as Ed drew his horse to a stop. He looked around, startled. Scowling, Ed dropped the reins, stepped to the ground, and hurried toward the kneeling man.

"Don't cut that steer, Lonnie. It's wearing a Skillet brand."

It's on my land!" Lonnie snapped. "I know it's a

180

Skillet steer. That's why I'm taking it. Mind your own business, Jessup. Morgan Hill is going to pay one way or another for what he's done. You may be scared of him, but I'm not."

His face contorted with anger, Lonnie Grayson started the knife on a downward sweep. Ed kicked him solidly on the shoulder and sent him sprawling backward on his haunches. A sharp command, a tug on the line, and the mustang let the rope go slack. Ed freed the steer and it ran away, bowing its back and kicking up its heels.

"Killing another man's beef is called rustling in these parts, Lonnie. They'll string you up for that."

Lonnie Grayson tossed the knife aside and scrambled to his feet. Knots of muscle worked along his jawline. His lips quivered and he looked like he was at the point of tears, but the expression was born of frustration and anger, not from fear. "My craw is full of you, Ed. I'm not going to take any more from you."

As he spat out the words, Lonnie's hands tugged at the buckle of his gunbelt. He laid the holstered Colt on the ground behind him and took a step forward, eyeing Ed's gun.

"You can fight with that weight on your hip or you can take it off," he said. "but you're sure as hell going to fight. I'm going to show you I'm not a man to mess around with."

Ed left the gun in place. He hooked his thumbs in his waistband and stared at Lonnie. "You don't want to do that, Lonnie. You've caught me at a bad time."

Lonnie forced a laugh. "You still playing like you're sick? Well, it won't work."

"I meant a bad time for you, Lonnie," Ed said flatly. "You've caught me when I'm in good shape

181

and ready to stomp anybody into the ground who bothers me, not like the morning you busted into my room at the Drover's Pride."

"That's another thing!" Lonnie shouted. "I owe you a licking for laying up with Ellen Ditmar."

Lonnie took off his cream-colored Stetson, laid it carefully atop the gunbelt on the ground, and assumed a fighting stance. Ed watched him with indifference. Lonnie bounced around on the balls of his feet like a boy preparing for a schoolyard fight. He tucked his chin in close to his left shoulder, pummeled the air with make-believe jabs, and made snorting noises through his nose.

Moving in a ragged circle, Lonnie took a step forward, feinted with his left hand, then stepped back. He repeated the maneuver three times, long enough for Ed to study his timing. So far Lonnie had not tried to land a blow.

The next time he stepped forward, Ed's knotted fist shot out to meet him. He hit him just above the belt. Lonnie doubled over with a soft grunt. Ed's other fist chopped down across the man's cheek, and Lonnie fell sideways to the ground.

He shook his head and stood up. Hunching his shoulders, he charged forward like a raging bull. Ed sidestepped his rush; then, as Lonnie turned to come back at him, Ed punched him squarely in the face. Lonnie sat down hard in the grass, blood trickling from his nose, then fell over on his back. He lay that way for a few seconds, then rolled over on his stomach. He put his hands against the ground and started to push himself up.

Locking his hands together, Ed straddled Lonnie's outstretched form and brought both fists down against the back of his neck. Lonnie groaned and went limp. His face was in the grass, his gasping breath blowing dirt away from his bleeding mouth. Still he struggled to rise, and Ed stepped away from him. He felt the urge to reach out and help him, but he knew Lonnie would resent it.

At last Lonnie got to his feet. His eyes were glassy and his curly brown hair hung in sweaty strands across his forehead. Blood and dirt streaked his face. Lonnie steadied himself, glared at Ed Jessup, and cocked his fists again.

Ed took a half step backward. "Let's quit this, Lonnie. You're just getting hurt for nothing. We're on the same side, remember? Let's save our energy for Morgan Hill, but let's wait for the right time."

Lonnie dropped his head to his chest, thought a moment, then abruptly turned his back. He picked up his hat, buckled on his gunbelt, and walked toward the mustang, coiling the rope which lay along the ground as he went.

Swinging aboard the mustang, Lonnie turned the horse westward where the burned-out shell of the Grayson cabin was barely visible in a shallow swale a half mile away. He looked back at Ed Jessup. "If we have to wait for Skillet to strike first, we ought to hurry it up some way . . . and don't think you've proved anything. We may be on the same side, but that don't make us friends. I'll get even with you. Count on it."

The fight had been so one-sided Ed felt somewhat ashamed he had been so vicious, but he still remembered the accusations Lonnie had hurled at him that day in the back room at Clayton's and the threats he had made when he found Ellen in Ed's room at the Drover's Pride Hotel. He had promised himself then that he would have the pleasure someday of whipping

183

Lonnie Grayson in return for those insults.

On his way back to his ranch he decided he would say nothing to Harve Grayson about the fight or the Skillet steer Lonnie was about to butcher.

While he was not working on the cabin, Ed decided it was a good time to take the mules and buckboard back to McPherson. Most of the heavy hauling was done. If he had to drag in more logs, he could manage with a couple of the horses running loose on the Triple J range. McPherson would charge him only a little for use of the mules and buckboard, but Ed needed to conserve what money he had left.

It was early afternoon when Ed reached Singletree's Main Street. The boardwalks were almost deserted, but he saw a few Sunday-dressed men and women leaving the Drover's Pride after a late lunch. Only two horses stood tied at the hitching rail in front of Clayton's Saloon.

"Well, a good howdy to you, Ed," McPherson said as Ed stopped the buckboard near the livery's office door. McPherson still wore his church clothes and was fidgeting uncomfortably in his white shirt, string tie, and frock coat. "Harve tells me your new place is coming along."

"Thanks to good neighbors." Ed smiled and climbed down from the wagon to stand beside the liveryman. "I came in to settle up with you, Adam."

While he was counting out the money to the liveryman, Harve Grayson came in from the dark maw which led to the stalls, a pitchfork clutched in one hand. He nodded a greeting, set the fork on the ground, and leaned against the handle. There was a smell of new hay and horse droppings about him, and he looked nervous.

After McPherson had pocketed Ed's money, Harve

184

Grayson asked, "Are you going to tell him about it, Adam?"

Ed looked from one face to the other. "Tell me what?"

McPherson looked off in the distance, his lips drawn tight. "Trouble, maybe. Looks like you're attracting strangers to you like a horse draws flies. Folks are still talking about you killing Milo Sloan, and now there's another hombre in town asking about you. He's a mean-looking cuss. He don't say much, but he carries his six-gun like most gunslicks do. He got in an hour or so ago. He left his horse and ambled off toward Clayton's."

"Did he give you a name?"

McPherson shook his head, jiggling the roll of fat beneath his chin. "After we looked into them eyes of his, we didn't want to ask."

Propping the pitchfork against the wagon bed, Harve Grayson freed the buckskin which Ed had led in by a rope tied to the tailgate. Grayson hoisted Ed's saddle from the buckboard, straightened the latigo straps, and had the buckskin ready for riding in a matter of minutes.

"You ought to get out of town and go back to the Triple J," Harve Grayson told him. "We'll need you if we're ever to make a stand against Morgan Hill and you can't do much good if you get yourself killed in a gunfight."

Ed's relaxed mood faded. His face sobered and his shoulders grew tense. "Just because a man asks a few questions doesn't mean he's looking for a fight," he said. He swung aboard the buckskin and lifted the reins. "I can't rest easy if I think somebody might be after me, and I don't aim to run from anybody ever again. I'll see who he is and what he wants."

He sat alone at a table a few feet beyond the far end of the bar—a lean, leather-faced man in a high-peaked hat, dark flannel shirt, and worn corduroy pants. A half-smoked cigarette dangled from the corner of his mouth. His eyes squinted against the smoke—eyes the color of wet limestone.

Ed saw him the moment he entered Clayton's Saloon. He stopped just inside the door for a few seconds and took a good look at him. He had no doubt that this was the man who had asked about him at the livery stable. The room was unusually quiet—so quiet Ed could hear Marshal Dan Plover smacking his lips as he bit into a sandwich at the other end of the bar.

Beside the marshal stood another stranger. He was a stocky, compact man in a buckskin shirt and what looked to be a pair of faded blue cavalry pants. He wore a set of matched Colts with buckskin thongs holding the holsters low on his thighs. Hair as black as a crow's wing hung down from beneath the sweat-band of his low-crowned brown Stetson. His eyes were equally dark.

As Ed started across the room toward the man dressed in black, Hal Clayton spoke to him. The saloon man was standing away from the bar, his back against the whiskey shelves. Sam Ditmar, his face solemn and pale, stood in a similar stance a few feet to the saloon man's left.

Ed saw their glance swing from him to the man dressed in black, then back again, as though they were trying to convey a silent message.

Clayton said, "Good to see you, Ed. I need to talk to you about something."

"Later," Ed said. From the corner of his eye he saw Marshal Plover wipe a hand across his face and start toward the door.

Looking covertly at Ed Jessup, the marshal said, "I'd best be getting out to the house, I reckon. Got a sick boy and Doc Stratton is coming by to see him directly. I ought to be there when he comes."

Ed raised his eyebrows, wondering why Plover felt the need to explain his abrupt departure. He watched the lawman's back disappear through the batwing doors, then moved over to face the man at the table. "I hear you've been asking about me."

The man nodded. "Sit," he said. His voice had the flat, hollow sound of a man with a bad cold.

Ed eased into a chair on the opposite side of the table, stretching his right leg so the black-handled Colt would be within easy reach.

"Name's Rio," the man said.

"Just Rio?"

"It's not even that. Real handle is George Brand. But I've been ridin' for one spread and another along the Rio Grande so long folks took to callin' me after it." He took the cigarette from his mouth and crushed it under his heel in the sawdust floor. "I'm here to kill the man who killed Jericho John Jessup. It's a favor I'd be proud to do."

The man's bluntness shocked Ed, and it showed in his eyes. Rio Brand spoke as casually of death as he might talk about the weather.

"That's a peculiar offer from a stranger," Ed said suspiciously. "Why would you want to help me? I never heard of you."

"It ain't for you," Rio Brand drawled. "It's for Jericho John. He done me a big favor once. I told him if he ever needed help all he had to do was holler, but he wasn't the kind to ask. About ten days ago somebody told me they saw a newspaper write-up about Jericho John bein' dead — somethin' to do with a difficulty with another rancher, I hear. It would pleasure me to put a piece of lead in the man who killed him. I'd feel better knowin' I finally had a chance to pay my debt to Jericho John."

"Care to tell me why you think you owe him?"

Rio Brand folded his hands on the table. "No, I wouldn't. I don't talk about that. Just tell me who needs killin'. I'll get the job done and you won't see me again."

Ed stared at the long, sharp-featured face, not sure Rio Brand was the kind of man he would want as a friend. He said, "There's a little more to it than just getting even. There are other people involved. A man named Morgan Hill and his Skillet crew are trying to run us off our land, and somehow we've got to hang onto it without bringing in outsiders. That would get me in trouble with the sheriff. I can't get into a range war, and I don't buy guns."

The only sign of offense was a stiffening of Rio Brand's slender back. "And I don't hire mine out," he said. He raised his glance to look toward the bar. "See that feller over there in the buckskin shirt? That's Apache Bob Cole. He was hitchin' his horse outside just as I come by. He heard what I heard, and he's here for the same reason. He owed Jericho John, too. Either of us is fast enough to gun down anybody you point to."

Chapter Sixteen

After catching Apache Bob Cole's attention, Rio Brand crooked his finger, motioning for him to join them at the table. The man in buckskins nodded and came toward them. His swift, gliding strides reminded Ed of a stalking cat.

Introductions were exchanged, and Apache Bob drew up a chair and sat down. His face was broad across the cheeks, tapering to a pointed chin. He had a quick smile that counteracted his sullen expression.

"I don't have a drop of Apache blood in my veins," he said. His voice was deep, resonant, and his speech was that of an educated man. "There's a little Cherokee in me, perhaps, but I'm mostly Black Irish and French. I was a cavalry scout, and those soldier boys like to scare the Indians by having one of their own. Some shavetail lieutenant started calling me Apache Bob, and I've been called that ever since."

"I told him why we're here," Rio Brand said.

Apache Bob Cole was more talkative than Rio Brand. He told Ed of a time when he was stranded in the desert, trapped under a dead horse that Comanche warriors had killed in a surprise attack. Jericho John Jessup had happened along in time to help.

"I've never seen a man throw so much lead," the

buckskinned man said, his black eyes narrowing with the memory. "He had two six-guns and a rifle peppering bullets at those Indians until they gave up and ran, then he hauled me forty miles to a doctor. I had a crushed belly and a broken leg. He walked half the time because his horse couldn't carry both of us. A stage driver over in Arizona Territory told me about Jericho John's death. I came as quickly as I could. I'd be willing to kill the man who's responsible for your father's death—more than willing."

Ed nodded, not surprised that news of John Jessup's death had spread so far. Stage drivers were like a prairie telegraph. They met each other at junction points, exchanging gossip, and news of any consequence was spread quickly along the frontier.

"My pa would be pleased to know you're here," Ed said, "but I don't know who actually killed him. I just know it was somebody from Skillet. That's Morgan Hill's place. I have to settle this thing myself. Part of the trouble is personal between me and Hill. Skillet's foreman, Brady Wayne, is the real troublemaker now, I think, but that's personal, too, so I can't draw you men into it. I don't want to. Hill would try to get the sheriff onto me for bringing in hired guns if I did."

Ed told them briefly of the events which led to his father's death. He admitted he was expecting more trouble now that he was rebuilding on Maverick Creek, but he insisted that Rio Brand and Apache Bob Cole not get involved. He thanked them for their offer to help and got up to leave.

"We'll just hang around town for a spell," Rio Brand murmured. "It might turn out you'll need us after all."

Apache Bob stood next to Ed, his eyes holding the stoic stare of an Indian now. "There'll be some more friends coming along. On my way into town I came across a camp about five miles out belonging to Jake Skinner and Caleb Malone. They'll be here to offer their help, too."

Ed gazed absently out the window, not sure of what he should say. He was puzzled, and somewhat flattered, at this unusual turn of events. A warm feeling swept through him, but he was depressed by the irony of the situation. These loyal friends of Jericho John Jessup, men his father had helped and had never spoken about, had ridden scores of miles to offer their help, while Ed's neighbors remained too afraid to challenge Morgan Hill.

"Caleb Malone," Ed murmured, searching his mind. "I've heard that name before. He's with the Rangers, I believe."

"Used to be," Apache Bob said. "He turned to ranching some years back. He and your father rode together at one time. You wouldn't have reason to know Jake Skinner. Jake's older brother was a banker down in Latimer. He was killed during a robbery. Jericho John tracked down the two hardcases who pulled the holdup and brought them in to hang. Word got around that he gave most of the reward money to the Skinner family. Jake was just a boy when it happened, but he never forgot it. It caused him to take up bounty hunting, and he's been at it for years. He's a good man to have on your side."

Ed nodded, but did not change his mind about declining their help. He told them good-bye again and went over to talk with Hal Clayton, knowing he would remember the hard, weathered faces of Brand and Cole for a long time.

The saloon man did not wait for him to reach the bar. Clayton walked to the door to the back room and Ed followed him. As soon as they were inside,

Clayton pushed his apron aside and withdrew a leather wallet from his hip pocket.

"Most of the time I keep my nose out of other people's business," Clayton said, "but I thought you ought to see this."

He took a folded bank note from the wallet and held it out for Ed to inspect. The edge of the bill was stained by a thin line of dried blood.

"That's part of my money," Ed said. "I bled all over it when Morgan Hill's men dragged me. Where did you get it?"

"A bunch of Skillet riders were in last night, drinking and whooping it up. They've finished their roundup and the old man let them have a night in town."

"Which one?" Ed asked softly.

"Brady Wayne," Hal Clayton said. "He bought a round of drinks for the crowd. This is what he paid with."

Ed felt his fingernails biting into his palms as he clinched his fists. "Did you tell Marshal Plover?"

Clayton nodded. "I showed him the bill, but he said it didn't prove anything. He said that Brady could have got it somewhere else, but he said he'd speak to Morgan Hill about it and let Hill handle it."

"I'll handle it," Ed said, turning to leave. "I'm not surprised it was Brady Wayne who jumped me in my hotel room. He must have heard about me carrying a lot of cash when I was buying up things to rebuild our house. I guess he figured I'd have to pull out if he took what I had left. Looks like he found a way to hire Milo Sloan's gun without it costing him a cent of his own money."

"Those two gents you were talking to at the table looked like hired guns, too," Clayton said pointedly.

"They're not. They were friends of my pa. They

want to help me fight Skillet as a favor to him, but I don't want them mixed up in it."

Clayton wiped his hands nervously on his apron. "They look like the kind who wouldn't wait for an invite if a fight started. What are you going to do?"

"I'm going to kill Brady Wayne. I can't get to him at Skillet, but I'll find a way."

Ed gave Hal Clayton a quick handshake and left. He did not glance again at Rio Brand and Apache Bob Cole as he went through the batwing doors and headed for his horse.

On his way out of town he met Matt Latham halfway along Main Street. Latham waved him to a halt, drawing his bay alongside Ed's buckskin.

"Adam McPherson told me you was in town. I was on my way to find you," Latham greeted him. He had dispensed with the suit he had felt obligated to wear while working at Lance Barker's General Store. He was back in range garb—Levi's, a hide vest, and a curl-brimmed black Stetson. An old steel-handled Colt was strapped to his thigh and a rifle butt protruded from the saddle boot next to his right knee.

"I'm fed up with store-clerking," Matt Latham said, a fiery glint in his eyes. "I'm going back to Maverick Creek with you. We'll get a roof on your cabin this week, then start on my place."

Ed smiled. "Good for you, Matt. Now that you've made a move, I expect the others will follow soon. Let's go home."

As they passed the Drover's Pride, Ed glanced at the dining room windows, wishing he could spend some time with Ellen Ditmar. He wanted to stop, but he rode on. After they had put the town behind them, Ed told Latham about his encounter with Rio Brand and Apache Bob Cole, and his decision not to accept their help. He then told him about the blood-

193

stained bill Brady Wayne had passed at Clayton's Saloon.

Matt Latham's short-cropped mustache bristled. "Why does Morgan Hill keep a skunk like that around?"

"Hill's got big plans," Ed said, "and Brady Wayne figures in them. I told you how Hill wants Molly to marry into the Wayne family so he can set up a partnership with Snaketrack and Roscoe Wayne, and how he wants to spread the Skillet brand all over the West."

"Yeah, you told us that when we had the meeting at Clayton's," Matt said, "but I reckon we're just about to spoil them big plans. He's not going to start with our land."

The talk stopped as the trail narrowed and they had to ride single file through a long stretch of brush. Ed led the way, twenty feet ahead of Latham. When they reached the open prairie again, they talked little, each preoccupied with his own thoughts. They were within a mile of Ed's new cabin when they saw a plume of brownish smoke rising from the ground, wafting into the cloudless sky. They stopped their horses, exchanging glances.

Matt Latham cursed. "Skillet!"

"Yeah, Skillet." Ed spoke through clenched teeth. "They're burning my place again."

Horses at a full gallop, Ed Jessup and Matt Latham sped across the grasslands. From the direction of their approach, the barn blocked their view of the cabin for a while. When they reached its shadow, Matt Latham lifted the rifle from its boot. Ed drew his Colt and cocked it. They pounded into the ranch yard.

There was no one in sight. They put away their guns and leaped to the ground. Flames five feet high were eating away at the logs around the framed-in front door. Dried grasses and brittle brush, gathered within walking distance of the cabin, were piled all along the front wall. The air was heavy with the odor of pitch as the soft pine logs fed the fire.

Their heads bent to shelter their faces from the heat, they clawed away the brush and grass to halt the spread of the fire. Then they ran to the barn, found buckets and an old tin tub, and hurried back to the well at the rear of the house. Matt Latham worked the pump handle while Ed carried bucket after bucket of water to slosh over the glowing logs.

As the fire slackened, they filled the large tub. Each held a handle on either side of it while they dumped out the water. Afterward, they shoveled loose dirt over the smoldering logs, and the fire was finally out.

They sat down on the pile of small poles Ed planned to use for roof beams. Soot smudged their faces, and trickling sweat traced lighter lines through it. They coughed spasmodically, trying to free their lungs of smoke and pine tar. Ed's arms and legs ached, and his chest heaved with fatigue.

He sat for a long time, his head lowered, his eyes staring at the trampled earth between his boots; then he stood up, drawing in deep breaths in an attempt to drown the anger which caused his pulse to echo in his ears.

"I'm going after Skillet, Matt." His voice was choked with anger. "If I had to fight Morgan Hill, I wanted to do it while I was defending what's mine — but I've had all I'm going to take."

Ed stared at the charred logs around the cabin entrance. It was fortunate they had arrived when they did. Had the fire spread to the corner joints, the entire structure might have collapsed. As it was, it would take two or three days of hard work to replace the portion which was burned.

"Ride back to Singletree and see if the others want to join us, Matt," Ed said. "I'll stay here to make sure none of these logs start burning again. Later I'll ride down to the flats where pa and I left some cattle bunched. Meet me there when you come back. Skillet might be watching this place."

Long before he could see anyone, Ed heard the rumble of hoofbeats. The sounds told him there were several riders not far away. Darkness had fallen more than two hours ago, but he had not risked a fire. He had eaten a meal of cold biscuits and dried beef he had brought from the barn where he had stored the things he had purchased in Singletree almost a month ago. He waited in the shadow of the cottonwoods which lined Maverick Creek.

A muted call broke the stillness of the night. "Hel-loo-o! Ed Jessup!"

He could see the shadowy outline of horses and riders coming along Maverick Creek from the east. There appeared to be at least ten of them.

"Over here, Matt!" Ed called.

He moved away from the trees and out to the lighter area of the flats. They came on faster, and soon there was the sound of creaking harness, stamping feet, and the blowing of horses around him. Leaving their reins trailing, the men dismounted and gathered in a circle.

"Should have been here all along," Clay Siler muttered. He stepped close to Ed, his black beard glistening in the starlight. "I reckon it took another fire to pull us all together, but we're all here. We found our hired hands scattered around town and brought them along, too."

Ed ran his gaze over the group. Sam Ditmar and

Harve Grayson were a few feet to his left, sur-rounded by six grim-faced, restless men, each with a rifle cradled in his arms. Ed did not know their names, but he knew if they were men who had rid-den for Grayson, Ditmar, Siler, and Latham, there would be no slackers among them.

Just past Ditmar's shoulder, he saw another face which startled him — a face lighter in color than the others, framed by silken hair and the collar of a yel-low blouse.

Ed pointed a finger at Sam Ditmar. "Why did you let Ellen come with you? This is no place for a woman!"

Ditmar looked toward his daughter. He shrugged and turned his palms upward in a helpless gesture. "I didn't let her. I couldn't stop her. You try giving or-ders to a girl like Ellen and see how far you get. She'll probably get herself killed, but I can't help it. If her ma knew she was here she'd skin both of us alive."

Anticipating that Ed would object to her presence, Ellen Ditmar had tried to fade into the background. Now she came forward, her dark eyes shining. Except for the yellow blouse, she was dressed much like the others. Ed saw a small handgun stuffed into the waistband of her Levi's.

"Before the night is over you might need somebody to tie bandages and clean up bullet wounds," Ellen said. "I want to help. Skillet burned my home, too."

"Then you'll stay here on the flats until we get back," Ed said "If anybody gets hurt, we'll bring them to you."

Ellen touched his arm and raised her face to look into his eyes. The warmth of her hand seemed to course through his body and his stomach quivered. "I'll do whatever you say, Ed. Just be sure you come back."

The irritation he had felt a moment ago was gone, and he squeezed her hand. He started toward his horse, then stopped and looked over the men again. Someone was missing.

"Lonnie Grayson has been spoiling for a fight since the first day I saw him," Ed said. "Why didn't he come along?"

The question was directed at Lonnie's father. Harve Grayson mopped his face with a bandanna and shook his head. "I couldn't find him. He must still be camped out somewhere around the home place. He hasn't been in town for three or four days."

Ed did not want to embarrass Harve Grayson by telling the group he had found Lonnie that morning trying to butcher a Skillet steer. It had been more than twelve hours since their fight, however, and Ed had expected Lonnie to sulk awhile, then ride on back to Singletree.

"I'll find Lonnie," Ellen Ditmar said.

"Stay here, Ellen," Ed said. "You can't do much looking in the dark, and it's not safe for you to be riding alone."

"I'll find him," Ellen repeated stubbornly, hurrying toward her horse. "I think I know where he is. There's a deep spring at the toe of a knoll about half-way between our house and the Grayson spread. Lonnie and I used to go on picnics there. It's a place he likes. He told me once he always hid out there after he had a run-in with his pa. I'm going to track him down and make him do his part to help."

Before Ed could protest further, Ellen waved and rode away. Ed shrugged helplessly, looked at the others, and said, "Let's ride."

As they left the flats, Matt Latham pulled his horse alongside Ed's buckskin. "I didn't want to go into it back there, Ed, but I ran into that feller Rio Brand you was telling me about. He was having a drink at Clayton's when I stopped in to tell Sam Ditmar about your plans. He heard us talking. Rio said there was a whole bunch of your pa's old friends in town. He said maybe he'd round them up and join up with us. Looks like there's a real gathering of fast guns in Singletree."

Ed scowled. "They've got no stake in this and I don't want them in it, Matt. It wouldn't look right . . . but they're the kind who'll do as they see fit. I'm glad they didn't show up before we got away."

"We might wish we had them with us before the night's over," Latham said above the thud of hoofbeats. "Skillet's got a lot of fast guns, too."

He pulled his horse away and the group rode on in silence. They crossed Maverick Creek near the spot where Ed had fought with Brady Wayne, and then they were on Skillet land. They had a two-hour ride ahead of them — long enough for tension and fear to play on their nerves.

It was possible the odds might not be as unbalanced as they appeared, Ed thought. Most of Morgan Hill's men would be fighting only because they were on the Skillet payroll. Some might pull out rather than fight, unwilling to risk their lives just to draw wages. Ed and his neighbors were fighting for much more. They were fighting for the right to live their own lives as they chose and prove they could not be trampled by the boots of a power-hungry range tyrant.

Shortly before midnight they topped the last of the rolling hills and looked down upon the narrow valley which sheltered the Skillet headquarters. Ed stepped from the saddle and the others swung down to stand around him. Ed wanted to review their plan. He also wanted to be sure every man among them was still willing to fight, and that no one had lost his nerve or changed his mind.

The strategy for the attack was uncomplicated. It would be suicidal to rush into the Skillet ranch yard with guns blazing at unseen targets. They needed to draw the Skillet men out of the buildings and get them into the open where Ed and his men would be. That would put the fighting on an equal basis.

"We'll burn a barn," Ed told them. "That'll stir them up and give us some light to shoot by. I know the layout, so I'll set the fire."

A murmur ran through the grim-faced men around him. The reluctance and uncertainty they had evidenced after Skillet's attack on their homes was gone now that a showdown was at hand. They were eager for revenge.

"I want to throw the torch," Clay Siler said. "When I think about how many times I backed down on things I wanted to do just because Morgan Hill didn't like it, it makes me sick. I was the first to join up with Ed. It was me that got the rest of you here. I ought to have the pleasure of setting the first fire."

Sam Ditmar and Harve Grayson put up similar arguments, both citing reasons why they should strike the first blow against Skillet. Ed found a way to settle the matter. He pulled up five stiff grass stems and plucked off the blades into varying lengths. He closed his hand, leaving the ends of the grass stems in view.

"We'll pull straws. The man who gets the short piece goes in and lights the fire."

Sam Ditmar won the draw. He stepped back and rubbed his hands together, pleased by the importance of his role. They had come prepared. Each man had stuffed a few rags in his saddlebags, and each brought a canteen filled with coal oil.

One of the riders broke some branches from a mesquite tree. Two torches were fashioned. Ditmar held them aloft and climbed aboard his horse.

"Set the first barn," Ed said. "The one farthest away from the corrals. Open the doors first so any animals that might be in there can get out. As soon as you set the fire, hightail it away from there. We'll move up closer and wait for you."

Silence hung over the group as Ditmar disappeared into the darkness. Signaling the others to follow, Ed moved briskly on foot toward the ranch yard. They left their horses behind so there would be less noise. Ed heard the click of metal and the scrape of leather holsters as the men checked their guns. All eyes were fastened on the scattered buildings before them.

The late moon had crept above the eastern horizon and the land was bathed in a silvery light. Except for the swishing of grass beneath their boots, everything was still. Ed studied the rambling structure of Morgan Hill's home. There were no lights showing — no sign of activity. The long shadow of the bunkhouse was just as dark and silent.

When they were within a hundred feet of the yard, Ed asked the men to spread out about ten yards apart to lengthen the line of attack.

"Don't shoot into the house," he warned. "Molly's asleep in there somewhere and I don't want her hurt. None of this is her fault."

The group broke apart, scattering to find whatever cover was handy — a dry wash, an outcropping of rock, or a cluster of brush. They waited, watching the nearest barn for some sign of Sam Ditmar.

Chapter Seventeen

Suddenly a match flared in the darkness, appearing no larger than the wink of a firefly. Then the flames flashed brightly at one of the rear corners of the building where Sam Ditmar had thrown his first torch beyond the view of Ed and the others.

There must have been loose hay there, for the fire grew rapidly, mushrooming upward and licking at the walls. A second torch flamed at the front of the building. It blossomed into an orange glow, and Ed saw Sam Ditmar's gangly silhouette, his long legs stretching into a run as he headed for his horse.

At that moment one of the Skillet riders came out of the bunkhouse, probably making a trip to the outside privy. Sam Ditmar was still in plain view, spotlighted by the light of the spreading fire. The man yelled, "Roll out, Skillet! Roll out! Get up! Somebody's burning us out!"

A shot rang out as Sam Ditmar was reaching for the horn of his saddle. His shoulders jerked and he crumpled to the ground. He did not stay down, however. He struggled to his feet, pulled himself into the saddle, and spurred away from the burning barn.

"Damn!" Ed breathed, and his first thought was of

Ellen, hoping she would not have to suffer the grief he had known.

For a few minutes confusion gripped Skillet headquarters. Men ran from the bunkhouse, tugging on their clothes and buckling their gunbelts. A lamp flickered inside the main house and Ed saw a shadow move across one of the windows. He was close enough to recognize the massive shoulders and tall figure of Morgan Hill.

Guns boomed as the Skillet hands ran from place to place, firing in every direction. Two men loped toward the barn and someone tried to call them back, warning them to stay out of the light, but it was too late.

A rifle cracked somewhere off to Ed's left, then another. One of the men in the firelight staggered and fell. The other one tried to grab him by the shoulders. Ed leveled his rifle, snapped off a shot, and the cowboy turned and ran. The man on the ground began to crawl toward the shadows, pulling himself along on his elbows.

The sound of a running horse, circling in the darkness behind him, caused Ed to whirl around, his gun raised. It was Sam Ditmar. He stopped the horse and slid out of the saddle. Ed ran to his side while Ditmar hung onto a stirrup strap with one hand.

"Hit me in the small of the back," said Ditmar, his face pale. "Just cut through some meat, I think. Didn't hit my rib bones. It burns like hell, though."

Grasping him by the shoulders, Ed eased Ditmar to the ground. A bullet kicked up dirt six feet in front of him and he ducked instinctively. The Skillet riders had shaken off their sleep and were fighting furiously. Someone had seen the flash of Ed's rifle and had fired at it.

He rubbed his hand along Ditmar's belt and drew it away with the dark sheen of blood in his palm. He scowled, flinching as more bullets whistled through the air above his head.

"You've got a hole front and back, Sam. The bullet went all the way through just above your hip, but that means a clean wound—no lead to dig out. How do you feel?"

Ditmar sat up, blinking his eyes. "Like a man who's just had a steer fall on him, but I'll get over it. I ain't bleeding enough to die. Maybe I can stuff my neckerchief under my shirt to help clot the blood. We're going to have to get moving or get killed. They're throwing a lot of lead at this spot."

Nodding, Ed bent low and ran toward the shadows of a brush clump. Sam Ditmar limped along behind him, breathing hard. Ed looked back toward the ranch yard. By now the barn was a giant roaring fireball lighting up the whole area. Morgan Hill, fully dressed, ran across the yard. He was waving a rifle over his head, and barking orders at his crew. His voice was clearly audible despite the noise from the guns and yelling men around him.

"Don't let the whole place go up in flames, you fools!" Hill stormed. "Watering troughs are all around you, and there are two wells in the yard. Wet down the other buildings or this heat will make them all catch fire!"

Four or five shots rang out from Ed's group, striking echoes from the nearby hills. Dirt and dust flew up around Morgan Hill. He dived into the shadow cast by an outbuilding.

"Missed that old hellion!" Harve Grayson growled. "Missed the chance of a lifetime to watch them sing hymns over him!"

Morgan Hill had reacted as Ed had hoped he would. He was trying to save his property, and that exposed his men. Skillet riders started scurrying

204

about, forming a bucket line to pour water on a barn and carriage shed. Ed nestled his rifle against his cheek, aimed deliberately, and fired at a moving figure in the firelight.

The Skillet man grabbed at his thigh and fell sideways. Moving the sight only a few inches at a time, Ed fired again and again. The noise around him hurt his eardrums as the other men also pumped lead at the Skillet crew. Powder smoke swirled through the air, the acrid odor stinging his nostrils. Screams of pain and tormented curses rose above the din. The Skillet men gave up the bucket brigade after three or four men fell from gunshots, and they took cover among the buildings again. Bullets swept through the grass and brush around Ed and the others.

Clay Siler crawled out of the darkness close by, groaning under his breath. Sweat dripped off his black beard. His right arm dangled at his side, blood running from his wrist.

"Somebody's going to have to truss me up some," he mumbled. "Dang near tore my arm off. Broke the bone, too. It's dead numb. Ain't much pain, but I can't hold a gun. Curt Slocum, one of my hired hands, is over there in the rocks. He's shot up pretty bad, too. Maybe we ain't proving much here after all, Ed. I think we bit off more than we can chew."

Caught up in the heat of battle and gratified by the chance to strike back at Morgan Hill, Ed Jessup had not considered the possibility of failure. A worried frown creased his brow as he ripped the seam of Clay Siler's shirt sleeve and looked at the bloody arm. He tore the sleeve off at the shoulder, folded it into a narrow strip, and knotted it around Siler's arm to stop the bleeding.

Guns continued to explode nearby, and he heard a man say, "Got another one, by damn!"

Ed said, "We've got three men hurt, Clay. Three out of eleven, and Sam Ditmar is still able to fight. Somebody was bound to get hurt, but we're showing Morgan Hill something. He's learning that Texas doesn't belong to him. It belongs to all of us."

The numbness was going out of Clay Siler's wound. Ed saw pain forcing tears into the corners of the bearded man's eyes. Siler lifted the mangled arm with his good hand and laid it across his lap as he sat on the ground. He shook his head. "I don't know, Ed. Maybe we ought to talk to the others. We've hit Skillet a pretty good lick. Maybe some of us would like to pull out while we can."

Before Ed could reply, another voice called, "Nobody who calls himself a man will pull out."

Ed looked around, surprised. Ellen Ditmar and Lonnie Grayson were standing a few feet away. Ed had forgotten about Lonnie Grayson.

Lonnie had his cream-colored Stetson pushed to the back of his head, his curly brown hair spilling down across his forehead. Excitement glittered in his eyes. He already had the notched Colt in his hand, swinging it around as his glance darted back and forth between Skillet and Ed Jessup.

"You're a little late," Ed said flatly, "but we can use your help. You'll need a rifle instead of a six-gun at this range. Some of the men brought spares." To Ellen he said, "I'm glad you're all right, but get back where you and Lonnie left your horses. It's safer."

As Lonnie Grayson turned to hunt for a rifle, Ellen grabbed his arm and pulled him back. It was only then that Ed saw the anger in her eyes. She said, "Not yet, Lonnie. Tell him what you did."

"We ain't got time for talk, Ellen!" Ed growled. "Get back like I told you!"

"You've got time for this!" Ellen said. She gave Lon-

206

nie Grayson a fierce kick to his kneecap as he tried to pull away. "Tell him, Lonnie!"

Grimacing in pain, Lonnie squared around to face Ed Jessup. He gave Ellen Ditmar a dark look from the corner of his eye, then blurted, "I burned your cabin. That's what she wormed out of me. I guess she's going to tell you if I don't."

Ed was squatting beside Clay Siler, but he was on his feet by the time the words were out of Lonnie's mouth. One quick stride put him in front of Lonnie Grayson. He slapped Lonnie fiercely across the cheek with his open hand.

Lonnie dropped the Colt and cocked his fists. Ed could see the mark of his fingers on the man's face, and the fury within him urged him to tear that face apart. Ellen stepped between them and shoved Ed away.

"I found Lonnie where I thought he'd be," she said, glaring at him. "His eyebrows were singed and his shirt was scorched. He wanted to do such a good job he kept piling on dry brush until the fire flashed up and got him. I had a bad feeling about that fire from the time I heard Lonnie was still hanging around out there. I made him believe I saw him do it, and then he admitted it."

Ed spat on the grass next to Lonnie's boots and turned his back on him. "I'll settle with you later," he said.

"You had it coming," Lonnie said lamely. "I told you I'd get even for that licking you gave me and for what — what I saw at the hotel. I wanted you to get off your butt and fight Skillet. I knew you'd blame Morgan Hill for the fire."

Ed did not reply. Clay Siler swore under his breath. "Hell's fire," Siler said. "We put the blame on Morgan Hill for something he didn't do."

Ed gave Clay Siler a withering glance. "Think about it, Clay. Where's your home? Where are your cattle? Lonnie didn't take them from you—Hill did that. We have to make a choice—either we make Hill back off now or we run. That's why we had to come here some day, Clay. Lonnie just pushed up the time."

Kneeling, he reached again for the tourniquet around Siler's arm, but Ellen Ditmar pushed him aside. "I'll look after him. You look after the fighting."

He nodded, picked up his rifle, and went off in the darkness to take up a position where his powder flashes would not draw fire in the direction of Clay Siler and Ellen. He stretched out in a shallow depression, his nerves edgy. There was a growing stillness in the night. While he had been talking to Ellen and Lonnie, the battle had fallen into a lull. Only an occasional shot came from the ranch yard, and there was little fire in return.

Ten feet away Ed noticed the outline of a hatted head. He opened his mouth to call out, but waited as the man rose to a stooped position and crept toward him. It was one of Latham's hired hands—a slim, cotton-haired man with a boyish face.

"Something's going on down there," the cowboy said. "I seen them bringing horses out of the corral and they've almost quit shooting at us."

The stillness worried Ed and he swung his glance uneasily around the land. At that moment the barn roof collapsed, sending a shower of red sparks spewing into the night sky. Fanned by the falling timbers, the flames brightened and lit up the ranch yard. Ed saw men working with horses and saddles at the far end of the bunkhouse. He could guess what was about to happen. Morgan Hill had lowered his voice and Ed could not hear his words, but the rancher was walking among his crew, giving orders.

"They're going to circle around in the dark and get behind us," Ed told the cowboy. "We're going to get caught between those on horseback and those who stay put. Pass the word on to the others. Tell everybody to open up with their guns and try to pin them down. If they circle us, we're finished."

The cowboy crawled away. Ed pumped shells into his rifle, aimed at the bunkhouse crowd, and fired three quick shots. Then the other guns started up and there was a steady roar in his ears. Fifty yards away, the horses began to buck and whinny. The Skillet riders, cursing and yelling, chased them around in an attempt to get them saddled.

After a few minutes of turmoil, the Skillet crew got the horses under control and the mounted men became a mass of moving shadows as they spurred away from the firelight, swung behind the bunkhouse, and began their circle.

Confident of Skillet's superior numbers, Morgan Hill's voice boomed through the night as he urged his crew to make haste. "It's that hardheaded Ed Jessup and them Maverick Creek ranchers out there!" he yelled. "Wipe them out once and for all! They wanted this war, and now they can die for it!"

Matt Latham came up beside Ed, his craggy face pale and haggard. "We're in a trap, Ed. What're we—"

Latham's voice trailed off as the rattle of gunfire came unexpectedly from the darkness on the far side of the Skillet buildings. Hill's riders had been out of view behind the bunkhouse for two or three minutes, but they had to cross another patch of firelight to start their circling maneuver. There appeared to be ten or twelve of them, all bent low in their saddles and whipping the reins around their mounts.

As they came into the lighted area a hail of bullets kicked up dirt around them. Horses squealed, men cursed, and there was disorder among them as the riders hauled back on the reins and everyone tried to turn at the same time. More shots sounded, and Ed heard the whirring whine of flying lead in the air. The Skillet men whirled as a group and spurred back to the shadow of the bunkhouse.

Ed turned to look at Matt Latham. Latham pushed his hat back and rubbed his mustache, a stunned look in his eyes. "Somebody else is shooting at Skillet! But who—"

Before Latham could finish the question, a far-off voice called out—a voice that sounded like it came from a man with a bad cold.

"Rio Brand here, Jessup!"

"Apache Bob Cole here!"

"Caleb Malone on this side, son!"

Names floated out of the night, identifying men Ed did not know and had never seen—Jake Skinner, Eli Musser, Luke Pettibone. . . .

Each introduction was punctuated by another burst of gunfire and the ranch yard was emptied of men as Skillet scurried for cover.

"I'll be damned!" Matt Latham breathed. "Your pa was one hell of a man, all them friends pouring in like this."

"Yeah," Ed murmured. "It's like pa got up from his grave to give us a hand." He was still somewhat awed by the unexpected intervention by Rio Brand and John Jessup's friends from the past. They had learned the location of Hill's ranch and had arrived at Skillet in time to catch Morgan Hill's men in a crossfire. It was not what Ed had wanted, but he had no control over the situation now, and he had to admit it might have been a disastrous night for the men from Maverick Creek if Brand had stayed in town.

A movement at the front of the carriage shed caught

Ed's attention. He raised his rifle and fired at the spot. Matt Latham lifted his gun and aimed at the same target. Ed flung his arm across in front of Latham, pushing the gun down. He said, "Wait, Matt!"

A pole jutted out from the doorway to the shed. A square of gray-white fabric which had been torn from a canvas wagon sheet dangled at the end of the stick. It began to bob up and down, reflecting the orange glow from the burning barn.

"Somebody's waving a white flag," Matt Latham said.

Ed nodded, a puzzled expression on his face. Morgan Hill's voice called out to him, "I know you're there, Jessup! Let me hear you!"

Ed Jessup cleared his throat, wanting his voice to be strong. "I'm here, Hill! What do you want?"

"I want to talk! Hold your fire! I've passed the word to my men! Hold your fire and come on in!"

The shots from the Skillet buildings stopped, and the Maverick Creek ranchers rested their guns. For a full two minutes Ed sat in silence, staring unbelievingly at the white flag in the Skillet ranch yard; then Morgan Hill stepped boldly into the open, a tall, square-shouldered shadow in the night.

Ed put his rifle down and rose slowly to his feet. The others began to gather around him, coming in from the cover of brush and dry washes. Clay Siler had fashioned a sling from someone's neckerchief and was carrying his bullet-torn arm in it, the fingers mottled with crusted blood. Farther back, Ed saw Ellen Ditmar with her arm wrapped around her father's waist. Sam Ditmar was leaning slightly forward to keep his balance. He was weak from the loss of blood, but he was still on his feet.

Seeing his eyes on her, Ellen frowned and said, "Don't go, Ed. It could be a trick. Make Hill come to

211

you."

"I have to go," Ed said. "I have to know if we can settle this thing peacefully." He turned on his heel and started walking toward Morgan Hill.

If Ellen needed any reassurance, it came from the darkness on the other side of the ranch yard. "We'll cover you from over here, Jessup!" Rio Brand called, adding as a warning to Skillet, "We'll hold our fire unless somebody makes a wrong move! If that happens, we'll be coming in, too!"

Ed left his rifle behind, but he kept his Colt. As he walked along he lifted it once with two fingers and let it drop back. The barn had been burning for more than an hour, and the fire was beginning to die down. Parts of two walls were still standing, defying the flames. The interior had dwindled to a bed of glowing embers. Most of the light now came from the moon, and the shadows in the ranch yard deepened.

Nodding brusquely, Ed took his eyes off the rancher and looked around him. His breath was tight in his chest and sweat glistened on his forehead. His eyes narrowed and his hand crept close to his holster as he saw the outline of the back of a man's head in the darkness at one corner of the carriage shed. All he could see was the edge of a white hat and a thatch of brass-colored hair shining in the moonlight.

"Don't worry about an ambush," Morgan Hill growled, following Ed's wary glance. "Five or six of my men are hurt. I told the other men to get them inside the bunkhouse and try to patch them up. People here do as they're told."

"Not everybody," Ed said. "Brady Wayne's over there in the dark." He looked into Morgan Hill's eyes. "I'm looking for a chance to meet Brady in a fair fight, but I'll shoot you first if he jumps me from behind."

Resentment flared in Morgan Hill's eyes. His lips

212

tightened and he said, "Forget about him. Brady just likes to be the last one to give up a fight. He'll go inside as soon as we leave." Hill turned and started toward the sprawling ranch house. "We'll talk inside."

"We can talk here."

"Inside," Hill rumbled, and did not break stride. Ed shrugged and fell in step beside him.

Chapter Eighteen

As they walked along the side of the house Ed noticed a sliver of light from Molly's bedroom. It came from a slight gap in the curtains which had been pulled across the windows. He recalled the look of ecstasy in her eyes during his fight with Brady Wayne and wondered why she had not been outside to witness the violence of the past hour.

A lamp was already alight in the parlor. Morgan Hill pushed the door open, held it for Ed, then closed it behind him. Hill crossed to the desk and dropped wearily into a chair behind it. He twisted at the big ring on his finger, a strange expression in his eyes as he studied Ed's face.

Ed remained standing. He ran his glance around the room. Animal heads looked down at him from the walls. Buffalo robes, wolf pelts, and deerskins lay on the wooden floor. Shadows changed shapes between the long open beams of the ceiling as the lamp wick sizzled and flickered.

"Are we stalling, or is this mess over?" Ed asked, still bewildered by Morgan Hill's surrender.

"It's over, Jessup." Hill's chin fell toward his chest and he sighed deeply. "Did you hear them names being called out? I heard them — Rio Brand, Apache Bob, Caleb Malone, Jake Skinner. I won't fight men like that. I won't risk taking the blame for their deaths. I didn't have any notion men like that would ever show up in Singletree. How did you ever find them?"

"They found me. They heard about pa's death and wanted to settle the score for him."

"Lord!" Hill breathed. His deep bass voice was low. The hard glint in the granite eyes softened. "I've got papers and pictures of all of them people. They're legends, every one of them, like your Pa. I should have left him alone, too. The fighting between us is over, Jessup."

It was hard for Ed to believe Morgan Hill was so awed by the presence of men who had earned their reputations with a gun — or perhaps he respected them because their daring had opened the way for men like him to benefit from the freedom of the frontier. The rancher rambled on, reciting their exploits from memory — Apache Bob Cole had scouted for Ranger captain Lee Ford on a mission to wipe out the Comanches on the Canadian River in fifty-eight; more recently, Rio Brand had fought along with Billy the Kid in the Lincoln County War, pulling out only when he decided neither side was completely honest in that bloody feud; Jake Skinner was known as the man who gunned down the notorious Buck Lacy on the streets of Victoria.

Hill knew a story about each of the men whose name he had heard, and he seemed eager to talk about them.

Ed was only half listening to Hill's droning voice. He was thinking about the rancher's earlier declaration that the fight was over, and that the Maverick Creek ranchers could return to their land in peace. The statement had sounded sincere.

Ed shifted uneasily in the chair and waited for Morgan Hill to stop talking, then said, "If you mean what

215

you say, I want it in writing. I want you to write out a paper saying you agree we have a right to the land north of Maverick Creek. Most of us have deeds to prove that, but we need to know you respect those deeds. You can put in that we know the south bank is the Skillet boundary."

Morgan Hill slammed his fist against the desktop. His heavy black eyebrows drew together in a straight line across his forehead. "I don't have to write things down. You've got my word and that's all you're going to get from me. You'd go around showing that paper to folks and bragging about it. I won't have that, but I won't bother you again. My word is good with everybody for a hundred miles around."

Ed rubbed his palms along the seams of his Levi's, studying the man's face. "All right. You're a bully of a man, Hill, but nobody's ever called you a liar. We'll take your word. I'll go tell the others."

As Ed turned to leave, the Skillet owner called, "Wait! I want to offer you another deal. I'll pay you four hundred dollars for Jericho John's guns."

Ed paused in midstride, his back stiffening. He felt like cursing the man, but he managed to conceal his disgust and said softly, "I buried them with him, but they wouldn't be for sale if I'd kept them."

"Too bad," Hill said. "They might have been in a museum someday."

At the door, Ed paused and looked back at Morgan Hill. "One other thing—I've got a score to settle with Brady Wayne. It has to happen. I'm pretty sure I heard his voice telling your men to shoot low enough to kill us the night my pa died, and I've got other reasons, too. I'm telling you this because I don't want you to take a hand in it when the time comes."

Morgan Hill's shoulders slumped and his jaw sagged to reveal slight jowls Ed had not noticed before. He looked old and tired.

"I know your reasons. Marshal Plover was out here about sundown today. He told me about Brady spending stolen money at the bar, and how he used the same stolen money to pay a hired gun. I don't hold with thieves. I read Brady wrong. I've given up on him. Right after the marshal left, I gave Brady his walking papers. I told him to pack his gear and pull out tomorrow." He sighed heavily and when he spoke it was as if he were talking to himself. "Skillet is about as big as it's going to be. I reckon I'll settle for that and just live out my days the way I am."

Hill rubbed his hand idly across the desk. "You and Brady can shoot each other to pieces if you're a mind to, but I don't want it to happen here. You'll have to find him after he leaves Skillet."

"I'll find him," Ed said; then he went out into the darkness. He felt relieved and satisfied. He could build his own ranch now, and he would not have to answer to the sheriff for starting a range war. Morgan Hill's word would settle that issue.

The stillness of the ranch yard was comforting. He welcomed the coolness of the night air against his face. He started to retrace the route he had followed with Morgan Hill, but changed his mind and walked around the other side of the house. For some reason he could not identify, he did not want to go near Molly's window again.

As he reached the open ground between the house and the glowing remains of the barn, Ed lengthened his stride, anxious to tell the other ranchers of their triumph. Grass rustled behind him and Ed halted abruptly, his pulse racing.

He knew who was following him in the darkness. Then Brady Wayne said, "Hold it right there, Jessup!"

Cold chills skipped across Ed's shoulders. He turned

around slowly, his right hand dangling near his holster. Brady Wayne stood thirty feet away, a rifle aimed at Ed's chest. He wore his big white hat, the brim casting a shadow over the golden curls which brushed against his shoulders. The fancy Colt with the silver inlays had been repaired. Ed saw the butt of it jutting out at a handy angle from Wayne's polished holster.

"Old Man Hill might be willing to let you walk away free, but I'm not." Wayne's voice almost choked in his throat. "Morgan's guts turn to sand when he faces up to somebody he's read about in the newspaper. He's got a notion he can be famous, too, if he can cotton up to enough fast guns. They don't count any more than spit with me. I don't like the deal he made."

"You don't know anything about the deal."

Brady Wayne forced a laugh. "You ought to know I don't miss much around here. After you and Morgan went inside I slipped around to the side of the house. The window was open and I heard it all. It won't do you a bit of good, Jessup. You can forget that agreement."

The light from the fire was about gone, and the moonlight cast deceptive shadows across Wayne's body. It was what Jericho John would have called bad shooting light. His stare fixing on the rifle in the man's hands, Ed walked deliberately toward Brady Wayne. At the right instant he wanted to be no more than twelve feet from the man. When he reached that point, he stopped and set his feet at a comfortable angle. He looked into Brady Wayne's golden brown eyes. They were as flat and indifferent as ever.

"Hill told me he fired you, Brady," Ed said quietly. He wanted to keep the man's fury alive, to rattle his thoughts and slow his instincts. "How are you going to change anything? You're not even welcome on Skillet any more."

The Skillet foreman tossed the rifle away. His skin

218

was dark beneath the hat brim.

"How are you going to change anything?" Ed repeated.

"By killing you." Brady Wayne's voice was a hoarse whisper. "That's what I should have done a long time ago. I'm not leaving Skillet. Some time in the morning I'm going to argue about the way Hill fired me. I'm going to make him mad enough to reach for a gun, then I'm going to kill him, too. When you're both dead, Molly will need somebody to lean on. She's going to think it's Hill's own fault that he got himself killed, and she won't hold it against me. I'll marry her and Skillet will be mine."

Ed shifted his weight slightly on one foot, his right shoulder moving forward in a line with Brady Wayne's chest. From the moment he had heard the Skillet foreman behind him, Ed knew he could not satisfy Morgan Hill's wish that he fight Brady Wayne in another place. It had to be here and now.

"You robbed me and hired Milo Sloan to kill me," Ed said.

A snort of disdain came from Brady Wayne. "I did that, all right, but that ain't the half of it. Now that you won't be around to tell tales, I can tell you — I killed your old man, too. That might have made me famous if I could have talked about it — famous enough for Morgan to respect. I'm the man who killed Jericho John Jessup. I saw his shadow against the window that night. I rode up close and cut him down. I figured you'd quit the country then, but you didn't, so now I'm going to cut you down the same way."

"Then do it!" Ed spat the words at him, feeling an overpowering hate for this boyish-looking, arrogant man who had brought him so much grief.

There was an animal swiftness to Brady Wayne. Ed had seen it in his graceful stride and in the way he carried himself. Now he saw it in Wayne's gun hand.

In daylight or darkness, the movement would have been only a blur. Wayne's shoulder twitched, a hand darted downward, and the silver-streaked Colt sprang into his palm. A tongue of blue flame flew out from Brady Wayne's fist and a deafening, lingering explosion rang in Ed's ears.

It sounded like one shot, but there were two. Ed had grown up in the same household with one of the fastest guns in Texas. He had been trained since boyhood not to think of the target in a gunfight, but to reach, lift, and fire in a single motion without hesitation. His bullet had already burrowed into the foreman's chest when Brady Wayne's shot went off. Ed felt the heat from Wayne's slug as it blew past his face.

Brady Wayne moved backward four steps, his booted heels dragging in the dirt. He fell on his back and his body quivered. His arms were stretched along the ground. Death spasms shook him, setting up strange reflexes that caused his fingers to keep squeezing on the gun. It had a hair trigger, and one more shot exploded from the jerking gun. The slug dug a harmless furrow across the ground, then Brady Wayne lay still, blood spreading a wet circle around the hole over his heart.

Men rushed from the bunkhouse and came running across the yard, yelling and cursing and swinging guns, but no more shots were fired when they realized the battle had not been renewed. They came to a halt a few feet in front of Ed Jessup, their guns lowered, their voices stilled by the sight of the dead man on the ground.

One of them spoke, and Ed looked up at him. It was Thad Lawson, the cowhand who had helped Brady Wayne drag Ed Jessup across the prairie. Ed recalled Lawson's reluctance to follow Morgan Hill's orders that day, and he felt no animosity toward him.

Ed had not moved from his tracks. He stood with his feet braced, the gun held down beside his thigh while he stared numbly at Brady Wayne's body.

"I knew it would come to this," Thad Lawson murmured.

Ed shook his head as if coming out of a trance. He holstered the gun and started to turn away. Someone brushed against his shoulder, then Molly Hill whisked past him. The Skillet riders stepped back to make a path for her. She was wearing a frilly white nightgown, but she had put on a pink satin robe to cover most of it. Her blond hair was in disarray. Her green eyes were bright with shock.

Without glancing at anyone, Molly ran to Brady Wayne's body and fell beside it. She looked down at the fixed stare of the brown eyes and cried, "My God, you've killed the only man I ever loved!"

Molly's shoulders convulsed. She lifted one of Brady Wayne's hands and hugged it to her breast. A shudder ran along her spine as she dropped the lifeless arm; then she straightened her back and stood up. She lingered a moment with her head bowed, her arms straight and stiff by her sides. Turning slowly, she came back to face Ed Jessup. There were no tears in her eyes.

A tentative smile parted her lips and she touched Ed's arm gently. "I don't know why I said that, Ed — why I said I loved Brady. You know it isn't true, Ed. You're the man I love. It's always been you."

Ed looked down at the beautiful face, a dubious look in his eyes. He shifted his arm so that Molly's hand dropped away, and searched his mind for something to say to her. Morgan Hill's voice cut across his thoughts, and he remained silent.

Hill had not been able to keep pace with Molly's flight from the house. He pushed through the circle of men. Hands on hips, he nudged Brady Wayne's body with the toe of his boot, then looked across at Ed Jessup.

"I told you not to fight him here," he said angrily. "Now I'm going to have to write a letter and explain things to his father, maybe the best friend I have on this earth — maybe the only friend. I see a gun in Brady's hand, so I believe it was a fair fight, but I asked you to settle your personal grudge somewhere else, not on my land."

"I had no choice. He forced a showdown."

Morgan Hill nodded. "I see. I'll tell his pa how it was." His voice was remarkably calm. He walked closer to Ed and slipped his arm around Molly's waist. "You've proved something to me, Jessup — you're more of a man than I ever thought. You've gunned down two fast men in just a few days. Milo Sloan and Brady Wayne. That could get you a reputation — maybe even make you as famous as Jericho John."

The big rancher paused and ran a hand through his hair. His eyes narrowed thoughtfully as he looked down at Molly's face, then again at Ed Jessup. "I've been hard on you two — even unfair, I guess. We're going to live together as neighbors and friends now, so it wouldn't matter to me if you and Molly decided to get married."

Ed stared solemnly at the rancher, and he felt his hands shaking. He said, "We'll live together as neighbors, Hill, but not as friends — not for a long time." He hesitated, then added, "As for Molly and me, well, we've been apart a long time and we've both changed. She — she wants more than I can offer."

Only now did he look at Molly. Her eyes were downcast, hooded by her long dark lashes. Her manner told Ed she knew he would not be calling at Skillet again.

He hurried away from the crowd in the yard. When he reached the deeper shadows beyond the barn, he called out for Rio Brand, Apache Bob Cole, and the others who had come to his aid. There was no answer. They had done what they came for and had melted into the night when it was over. They had paid their debt to Jericho John. Ed would not see them again.

The tension had run out of him and he felt tired, worn out. He went back to the place he had left his rifle, but the shallow depression in which he had knelt to fire at Skillet was deserted. The Maverick Creek people had withdrawn to wait with the horses. He headed in that direction and presently he saw Lonnie Grayson standing in a patch of moonlight ahead of him.

'When Ed came abreast of him, Lonnie handed Ed a rifle and said, "I picked this up and held it for you. We figured things were going all right down there, so we went back to check on the horses. Ellen wanted to get her father to a doctor. Clay Siler and one of his hired hands need looking after, too, so everybody started on to Singletree. They said they'd meet you there. I came back when I heard the shooting."

Nodding, Ed took the rifle from Lonnie's hands and cradled it in the crook of his arm. He thought about the time he had spotted the campfire on his land, and had spent half the night trying to run down an intruder. He knew now that Lonnie had scouted his place more than once before the fire, and that the tracks he found around his cabin the next day were left by Lonnie's horse. Too much had happened for Ed to develop any new grudges, and his harsh feelings toward the man were beginning to fade.

Ed told Lonnie about Morgan Hill's agreement, and of the gunfight with Brady Wayne. He dropped to the ground to rest a minute. Lonnie sat down beside him.

The curly-haired youngster scraped dirt out of the grass with his boot heel. "That was a damn' fool thing I did, Ed — burning your cabin, I mean. I'll help you build it back."

223

Ed glared at Lonnie, anger dancing in his eyes. "You sure as Satan will, or I'll stomp you into the ground."

"I'll help, I'll help!" Lonnie said quickly. He ran his tongue across his lips and shook his head. "Hearing about that fight with Brady Wayne and knowing how fast you are makes me feel like a fool."

"What do you mean?"

"This notch on my gun—it ain't real. It don't stand for nothing. I never killed anybody in my life. I just cut it on there to look tough and get some girls to notice me."

The sober expression on Ed's face softened. He grinned. "I'm not surprised, Lonnie. You've always been a show-off. Just try being yourself and you'll get along fine with women—maybe even Ellen Ditmar."

His reference to Ellen was meant to test Lonnie's feelings, and he spoke it with misgivings. Lonnie chuckled dryly. "No chance of that, and you know it. Ellen has already told me once tonight she wouldn't have me if I was the last man on earth. She said she was going to marry you if you ever ask her."

Ed rose and walked toward the horses. Lonnie trailed a step behind him. "Well, she's sure going to get asked, Lonnie. She's going to get asked before the night is over."

Ed's spirits lifted and there was a spring in his stride. It seemed years since he had laughed out loud, but he laughed now, and it felt good. The buckskin would be rested, ready for a fast gallop, and Ellen Ditmar could not be very far along the trail to Singletree.

BC	10|12
KE	04/23